A visit from the undead . . .

Johnny's jaw fell open as he stared into the darkness. From the deep gloom someone was coming toward them—someone or something. It was as tall as a man, but it moved with a shambling, loose step, as if it were about to fall apart.

It was a walking skeleton, dressed in the flaking scraps of a Pilgrim suit, with a tall, conical hat atop its pale, grinning skull. Ancient, dried shreds of moldy green flesh stuck to its cheeks, and cobwebs busy with spiders filled its eye sockets. The long, tattered coat that it wore hung open, and inside the skeleton's rib cage gray shapes moved, huge, red-eyed rats that gnawed the bones with their yellow teeth. The skeleton thrust its arms out as if it were blind in the light, and Johnny saw that its left hand was missing. The shape lurched forward, its jaws gaping, a hollow groan coming from its bony mouth. . . .

PUFFIN CHILLERS BY JOHN BELLAIRS

Johnny Dixon Mysteries
The Curse of the Blue Figurine
The Mummy, the Will, and the Crypt
The Secret of the Underground Room
The Spell of the Sorcerer's Skull
The Drum, the Doll, and the Zombie
The Revenge of the Wizard's Ghost
The Eyes of the Killer Robot
The Trolley to Yesterday
The Hand of the Necromancer

Lewis Barnavelt Mysteries
The House With a Clock in Its Walls
The Figure in the Shadows
The Letter, the Witch, and the Ring
The Ghost in the Mirror
The Vengeance of the Witch-Finder
The Doom of the Haunted Opera

Anthony Monday Mysteries
The Dark Secret of Weatherend
The Treasure of Alpheus Winterborn
The Mansion in the Mist

The Hand of the
Necromancer

John Bellairs's
JOHNNY DIXON *in*

The Hand of the Necromancer

by BRAD STRICKLAND

Frontispiece
by Edward Gorey

PUFFIN BOOKS

PUFFIN BOOKS
Published by the Penguin Group
Penguin Putnam Inc., 375 Hudson Street, New York, New York 10014, U.S.A.
Penguin Books Ltd, 27 Wrights Lane, London W8 5TZ, England
Penguin Books Australia Ltd, Ringwood, Victoria, Australia
Penguin Books Canada Ltd, 10 Alcorn Avenue, Toronto, Ontario, Canada M4V 3B2
Penguin Books (N.Z.) Ltd, 182-190 Wairau Road, Auckland 10, New Zealand

Penguin Books Ltd, Registered Offices: Harmondsworth, Middlesex, England

First published in the United States of America by Dial Books for Young Readers,
a division of Penguin Books USA Inc., 1996
Published by Puffin Books,
a member of Penguin Putnam Books for Young Readers, 1998

1 3 5 7 9 10 8 6 4 2

THE LIBRARY OF CONGRESS HAS CATALOGED THE DIAL EDITION AS FOLLOWS:
Strickland, Brad.
The hand of the necromancer / by Brad Strickland.
(based on John Bellairs's characters)
frontispiece by Edward Gorey.   p.   cm.
Summary: Thirteen-year-old Johnny Dixon and his friend Professor
Childermass battle an evil wizard for possession of a bewitched
hand that can be used to rule the world.
ISBN 0-8037-1829-2 (trade).—ISBN 0-8037-1830-6 (lib. bdg.)
[1. Wizards—Fiction. 2.Magic—Fiction. 3. Mystery and detective stories.]
I. Bellairs, John. II. Title.
PZ7.S9116Jo 1996 [Fic]—dc20 95-47222 CIP AC

Puffin Books ISBN 0-14-038695-5

Printed in the United States of America

In memory of Fred Johnson,
a wonderful teacher, a wonderful friend

CHAPTER ONE

"It's gonna be a rotten summer," said Johnny Dixon. "Fergie will be away until August, and my dad can't come home until Christmas. There's nothing at all to do."

Professor Roderick Childermass overcame an urge to snap at his young friend. It was a perfect June day in the 1950's, and the two of them were sitting in kitchen chairs on the professor's porch, a chessboard on a folding table between them. The professor was an elderly man with a nest of white hair, wild muttonchop sideburns sprouting from his cheeks, and a pitted red nose like an overripe strawberry. He glared through his gold-rimmed glasses at Johnny, a short, bespectacled, blond, freckled boy of about thirteen. "Hrrmph," growled the professor.

"Nothing at all to do, eh? Well, John, I suppose that you're just here playing chess with me out of pity. It's not that I beat you four times out of six or anything, is it? You just want to humor a crabby old man."

Johnny looked more miserable than ever. "Aw, no, Professor," he said apologetically. "I like playing chess with you. It's just that—well, I was hoping that Dad and I could take our fishing trip in Florida soon, and then he wrote to say we couldn't. Fergie said we were going to work on my batting and fielding this summer, but then his grandmother got sick. Fergie and his mom had to go to Ohio to take care of her, and—and I don't really have any other friends my age, and—oh, I'm sorry."

"Apology accepted." The professor stared at the board, then moved a black knight to threaten one of Johnny's bishops. As Johnny thought about his next move, the professor reflected that his young friend really had some cause for complaint. Johnny was brainy, but he was lousy at sports, and he did not make friends easily. Once a week he went to his Boy Scout meetings, but as often as not the other boys ignored him or played mean tricks on him. Johnny's mother was dead, and his father was off in the Air Force, training Strategic Air Command pilots, so naturally the boy was lonely. He lived with his grandparents across from the professor on Fillmore Street in the town of Duston Heights, Massachusetts. Henry and Kate Dixon were kindly and loved their grandson, but like the professor, they were old. Sometimes young people like Johnny just wanted to hang around with someone else their age. "What exactly is wrong with Byron's grandmother?" asked the professor.

Johnny moved a pawn to protect his bishop, heaved a deep sigh, and sat with his chin resting in his hand. "She fell and fractured her hip. The doctor thinks she's gonna be okay, but it will take a long time for her to get well again. Mrs. Ferguson went out to Ohio to stay with her until she can take care of herself, and Fergie had to go along to help with chores and stuff." Byron Q. Ferguson—"Fergie" for short—was Johnny's only close young friend. They shared a love for historical trivia and a taste for gooey chocolate treats at Peter's Sweet Shop downtown. Fergie, though, was the more adventurous boy. Often Fergie could talk the somewhat timid Johnny into escapades that sometimes landed the two friends in serious trouble. On the other hand, with Fergie around, it was hard to be bored.

Professor Childermass reached to move a rook. For the first time he noticed that if he did, he would open his king to a double-pronged attack from the marauding bishop and from Johnny's queen. "Very clever," he growled, glaring at the chessboard. "Hrrmph. All right, you sneak, you got past my defenses that time. I resign." The professor tipped over his king to show defeat. Then he leaned back and reached for one of his black-and-gold Balkan Sobranie cigarettes and his Nimrod pipe lighter.

"Uh, Professor?" said Johnny, a grin on his face. "Remember, we have a deal. You can smoke only when you *win* a game."

For a second the professor looked cranky and cross. He had an explosive temper, and he terrified practically everyone in Duston Heights. However, he almost never blew up at Johnny. The old man and the young boy had an odd, unlikely friendship, but it worked. Instead of snarling or snapping, the professor simply replaced his cigarette box with the air of a martyr. "Sooner or later I am going to give up this filthy smoking habit, and then you will have nothing to hold over me," he muttered.

After a moment he added slyly, "John, it seems to me that what you need is a good, honest summer job. Maybe you could work, oh, four hours a day. That would keep you busy, and you could earn money for a Red Ryder air gun or a Super Spy camera or whatever it is boys your age need money for these days."

"Where am I going to find a job?" asked Johnny, his voice discouraged.

"Leave that to me," returned the professor with a grin. "Come along, my fine feathered friend, and I believe I can promise you gainful employment." He rose from his chair and went inside his big, gray stucco house.

Johnny followed the old man upstairs to the cluttered study. The professor's desk overflowed with blue books containing final exams from the spring term at Haggstrum College, where the old man taught history. A stuffed owl wearing a miniature Red Sox baseball cap sat on a round stand by the desk. It stared at the two with glassy yellow eyes. The professor opened the door of a small closet, which he called his fuss closet. It was where he always went when he just had to be alone to rage and rave and stomp around to get some anger out of his system. He had lined the closet with padded gymnasium mats to keep the noise down and had tacked a hand-lettered sign to the back wall: To Fuss Is Human; To Rant, Divine!

On the closet floor was a big cardboard box full of odds and ends that lay jumbled together. The professor lifted the box, took it to his desk, and swept off a drift of papers to make room for his burden. "There," he said, setting the container down with a thump and a rattle. "John, did I ever tell you about Esdrias Blackleach, the weird wizard of Duston Heights?"

Frowning at the box, Johnny shook his head.

"Well, he was one of Duston Heights' earliest settlers. To be perfectly accurate, he settled in a small village called Squampatanong, which is what Duston Heights was called before it was renamed for Hannah Duston. Anyway, you might remember that down in Salem Village in the early 1690's there was a bit of an uproar about witches, warlocks, and wizardry."

"The witch trials," said Johnny. "They hanged a bunch of people who were accused of sorcery."

"To be exact, they hanged nineteen men and women who were condemned as witches. That's not counting a twentieth victim, stubborn old Giles Cory. The court officials pressed him to death by putting him beneath a barn door and piling stones on it until he was crushed. He doesn't really count, though, because his case never came to trial. Well, my boy, at the same time as that little hullabaloo, witchcraft hysteria broke out all over New England, even up here in the hinterlands north of Boston. At that time there were only about one hundred and fifty souls in Squampatanong, and of them a round dozen were accused of witchcraft and imprisoned."

"I haven't heard about that," confessed Johnny. He was itching to find out what lay inside the mysterious cardboard box.

The professor seemed to be in no hurry to satisfy Johnny's curiosity. "I'm not surprised. The episode never got to be as famous as the Salem trials. Fortunately for our town's good name, none of the accused witches were actually hanged. It's a safe bet that none of the citizens of the little village ever dreamed of practicing witchcraft. All but one, anyway: the infamous Esdrias Blackleach. Legends say Blackleach was a genuine, honest-to-badness wizard, or at least he tried to be, though he was never brought to trial. People had just begun to suspect him of witchcraft when he suddenly dropped dead of natural causes. That was a couple of months before Governor William Phips put an end to all the witchcraft trials by decree."

"Professor," said Johnny, "all this is very interesting, but what does it have to do with my getting a job?"

"Patience is a virtue, John," the professor reminded him. "But let me make it all clear. You remember the summer we spent up at my wacky brother Peregrine's estate in Maine, don't you?"

Johnny shivered. The late Peregrine Childermass had been something of a nut—a rich nut, but loony as a bedbug nonetheless. Peregrine Childermass' estate on Lake Umbagog was a bizarre old place with crumbling towers, sinister statues, and a mysterious tomb. His attempt to use magic to bring comets swooping close to the earth was meant to scare all the nations of the world into peace. Unfortunately, an unscrupulous wizard poisoned Peregrine, swiped his spell, and nearly succeeded in bringing the world to a fiery end. "I remember, all right," said Johnny through clenched teeth.

"I never told you that Peregrine left me this charming assortment of bric-a-brac. These items once belonged to Esdrias Blackleach, and my silly sibling bought them all at auctions over the years."

The professor began to unpack a remarkable heap of junk from the box: three corroded iron balls joined to each other by chains; a snow globe with a house, trees, and a human figure inside; a thin, age-blackened wooden wand; a tarnished hand mirror about three inches across; a small book protected inside a cardboard sleeve; some tiny faded cloth dolls; a wood carving that looked like a life-sized human hand; and other things. "Professor," complained Johnny, "I *still* don't see how all this is going to get a job for me."

"Elementary, my dear Dixon," returned the professor. "For months the Gudge Museum has been after me to lend this weird conglomeration to them. I haven't done it because, frankly, I don't much like Miss Ferrington, the curator. Then too, I didn't want to go to the trouble of packing all this junk up for the benefit of a bunch of yokels who will gawp at it and tell one another how simple-minded our ancestors were. However, since the museum is so anxious to display this unsavory reminder of our town's past, and since I happen to know that its janitor has just retired to Florida, I think a little quid pro quo is in order."

Johnny grinned. He was good at Latin, and he knew that "quid pro quo" meant a trade, getting something you want in exchange for something you have. "So you'll lend this stuff to the museum if they hire me."

"Exactly. Is it a deal?"

Johnny picked up the so-called snow globe. It was not a true globe or even a dome, but was flattened at the top, like the bottom of a drinking glass. The greenish glass was thick, with bubbles and wavery lines in it. And inside the container was a little human figure, so bundled up that you couldn't tell whether it was a man or a woman. It strode through the snow toward a small log hut. A few faded green cones suggested evergreen trees. Johnny shook the globe, and the fake snow swirled.

The professor picked up the carved hand. "Now, this is a strange piece. In fact, of all this mess, this carving seems to me to be the most uncanny."

Johnny put down the snow globe and stared at the

carved hand. "It looks like a form for a left-handed glove."

"Ah." The professor put the hand on the desk. It rested on its cutoff wrist, as if it were waving. The wood was a light brown, with a wavy darker grain in it, something like maple. The fingers were slightly spread, and the thumb stood out at a normal angle. "This is the only item left by the old wizard that ever gave me nightmares. Soon after it came here from Perry's estate, I had some doozies, so I packed it away with the other cute little mementos and forgot about it. Touch it if you want."

Johnny picked it up. The carving felt surprisingly light, not like solid wood at all. He was turning it in his hands when Professor Childermass said, "According to the old stories, that hand is the last work ever carved by old Esdrias Blackleach of Squampatanong—good heavens!"

Johnny cried out and flung the hand away from him. He jerked his arms convulsively, knocking the snow globe to the floor with a loud crash. The hand spun on top of the desk and fell off onto the professor's lap. At that moment Johnny could not even speak, but merely stood there gasping.

For at the mention of Esdrias Blackleach's name, the wooden hand had suddenly closed its fingers on his own, giving him a ghastly handshake.

CHAPTER TWO

The professor's plan to help Johnny get a job came off with only two minor hitches. First, Miss Ferrington agreed to take Johnny on only temporarily, until he proved that he could do the routine work in the museum. Johnny thought that would be no problem. Mr. Haskins, the old janitor, had worked until he was eighty-one. In Johnny's opinion, if he couldn't do at least as much dusting, sweeping, and mopping as an eighty-year-old man, he just wasn't trying.

The second small change in plan was that Professor Childermass let Miss Ferrington have everything except the carved wooden hand. After Johnny's experience, the professor was suspicious about its innocence. Although Johnny and he had tried several times to make it move again by mentioning Esdrias Blackleach's name, it remained just a dead piece of wood. Johnny began to wonder if he had only imagined its movement. Still, the professor decided he had better investigate the relic more fully.

Johnny began work on a Monday morning. His trial period would be one month, and during that time he would earn ten dollars a week for working four hours a day, Monday through Friday. He began to ponder what he could buy with the extra cash.

For a week everything went well. Or as well as could be expected with Miss Ferrington as his boss. She was a sour-faced woman who kept her steel-gray hair in a tight bun, and she peered at the world through thick glasses. She always complained about something, and even when she could find no fault with Johnny's work, she would never compliment him. A frosty "Hmpf, I suppose that will do" was as much as he could expect from her.

The Gudge Museum was a Federal-style building on the north side of West Merrimack Street. It had been built in 1790 as the home of Parson Randolph Gudge of the First Congregational Church, and later became the home of the parson's granddaughter, the poet Sophonsoba Peabody. In fact, Johnny thought, if Miss Ferrington had her way, the museum would be *called* the Museum of the Great, Wonderful, Underappreciated American Poet Sophonsoba Peabody.

Sophonsoba Peabody had lived from 1812 to 1886, and Miss Ferrington was a descendant of hers. Miss Ferrington did not care about any part of the museum except the Sophonsoba Peabody Room, and she was always trying to buy furniture and clothing and personal articles that had once belonged to old Sophonsoba. Sophonsoba had written long, soupy poems about Nature and Selfless Love. She had known the Massachusetts poet John Greenleaf Whittier, who even in old age used to run three or four blocks out of his way to avoid having to talk to her. The room dedicated to her memory was crammed full of delicate, fragile items that absolutely could not be touched but that had to be kept clean. Johnny could do without the Peabody Room, though he liked most of the other exhibits in the museum.

The professor's boxful of witchy items, minus the wooden hand, wound up on the third floor of the museum, in the Colonial Curiosities Room. This room was the only display area on the stuffy, dusty third floor, where all the other rooms were storage spaces. The Curiosities Room displayed Colonial household items and homemade crafts on shelves and tables, and the Blackleach exhibit had a whole set of shelves to itself. The walls were decorated with antique framed quilts that pioneer women had stitched by hand.

At 1:00 P.M. on Friday, Johnny had just finished dusting the Curiosities Room, which he privately called the Witch Room. This was his last task before he would receive his very first pay envelope. He put up his broom, dustpan, and feather duster, wondering what he would do with all that money.

He paused before the Blackleach shelves and picked up the snow globe. It now had a card in front of it reading:

Handmade Snow Globe
Made by the Early Settler
Esdrias Blackleach, 1690.
(This Is the Earliest American Example of
This Type of Craft).

Since Johnny had knocked the globe off Professor Childermass' desk, it had an additional feature. This was a hairline crack where the glass joined the wooden base. It was not more than a half-inch long and almost invisible. The crack did not appear to go all the way through the glass, because no water was leaking out.

Well, at least the globe still worked. Johnny inverted the snow dome, swirled it, and watched the blizzard sweep around the poor traveler inside. The little figure was too small to have a real face, but somehow Johnny imagined it with a look of terror as it desperately tried to reach the safety of the log cabin. Something was after the fleeing figure, something horrible rushing from the woods. It was bounding along on silent paws, and its slavering jaws gaped open to—

"Ah, another fancier of Colonial antiquities."

The sly, hoarse voice made Johnny jump a mile and almost made him drop the globe a second time. He thrust it back on its shelf and spun to confront the visitor, who had come silently up behind him. The man was skinny and tall and completely bald, with dark, deep-set eyes. He wore an old black suit, a white shirt that looked faintly yellow with age, and a narrow, black silk tie. He smiled, showing a mouthful of crooked, brown-stained teeth. "My," he said in his hoarse voice, "what an industrious young fellow, tidying up the exhibits, hmm? Do you, by any chance, ah, work here, young man?"

Johnny swallowed hard and nodded.

"Ah, wonderful," the stranger grated. "I understand that somewhere in this establishment are some, um, um, curiosities? Am I correct?"

"Well, we have a lot of exhibits," Johnny said. "There's the Colonial Life Room on the first floor, and the Sophonsoba—"

"Bah!" The stranger almost spat the word out. Then he gave Johnny another twisted smile. "No, I mean ar-tifacts specifically related to, ah, um, the practice of witchcraft."

"S-sure," Johnny stammered. "Th-this is the Wi—I mean, the Curiosities Room. We have some things that used to belong to Esdrias Blackleach."

The strange man smiled a ghastly smile. "I know that name. Wonderful."

"Well, I have to go now—"

"No, no. Stay and tell me about these delightful ex-hibits." With a sudden convulsive movement, the man's hand closed on Johnny's wrist. "Tell me, you clever boy, what is that?"

He had pointed to a big leather-bound book on a dictionary stand across the room. It was open, its liver-spotted pages almost glowing in the daylight shining through the north windows. "Uh, that's the Hathorne diary and daybook," Johnny said. "It's a rare printed copy of a diary kept for more than twenty years by John Hathorne of Salem Village—"

"A remarkable man," grated the stranger. "Old John Hathorne! Others repented of the witchcraft trials, but not John! He had a spine of steel, that one. It was he who boasted of whipping a Quaker woman half to death and then casting her out to die in a snowstorm. A quick one to sniff out witchcraft was good old John Hathorne. And what is that interesting display, hmm?" The man dragged Johnny about the room, demanding answers about this and that. His eyes glittered as he caught sight of the snow globe. "Bless my soul," he said. "Unless my eyes deceive me, this is one of the works made by Esdrias Blackleach, hmm? Ah, yes, so the card says."

"Yes, sir," replied Johnny. He was desperate to get away. "It's a sealed glass snow dome mounted on a maple base—"

"Ash!" the strange man said almost in a hiss. "It's ash, not maple. It makes a difference in the conjuring. Old Esdrias was far too cunning in the knotty ways of the Secret Arts to make such an elementary mistake. A pretty bauble, is it not, hmm? A soul could stare into that snow and lose himself. To think that it's almost three hundred years old. The cold drifts that old Esdrias stirred are still blowing, eh? Still sweeping souls before them? What else of his do you have?"

Johnny looked around. "Well—he made the hand mirror there. And the snuffbox and the wand beside it. There are some unidentified implements that he owned on the top shelf. And he carved some scrimshaw—"

The man gave Johnny's arm a painful half twist. "These are minor! These are playthings. What about his greatest work, hmm? Where is that, my boy?"

"I don't know what you mean!" It came out as a terrified squeak.

"Don't you indeed? It is a hand, my fine young man. I hear he carved a very pretty hand while on his deathbed. You have it here, somewhere, don't you?"

"No!" Johnny said, trying to pull his wrist away. "Please, let me go. I have to—to go downstairs. There's a—"

"Not here?" the man said, his face turning purple. "It must be here! I've checked every other place. Every place except for one." He fell silent, glaring at Johnny. "I understand there is a man in town named, what was it? Childerman? No, I have it now, Childermass. Professor Roderick Childermass. He and I have much in common. We are both enthusiasts. I'm sure you know the good professor, do you not?"

The hand on Johnny's wrist was clamping tighter and tighter, like a constricting snake squeezing, squeezing, cold and deadly. Johnny dared not speak, but he shook his head. It was not exactly a lie, perhaps, but the strange man thought Johnny had answered his question.

The hand let go at last. "No?" The bald stranger hissed between his bad teeth, and then he said, "Well, Duston Heights is a small town. I'm sure I will find him soon enough. He and I will have many interesting subjects to discuss—"

Out in the hall the stairwell door opened, and a moment later Miss Ferrington came in, speaking over her shoulder to a group of six or seven bored-looking high-school students who were suffering through summer school. "And the Curiosities Room," she was saying. "So called because it offers many unique and absorbing exhibits from the superstitious days when—Johnny Dixon! Why are you still here?"

Johnny was happier to see her than he had ever thought possible. "Miss Ferrington, this man wanted me to show him—"

"Your duties do not include leading tours," Miss Ferrington snapped. "You will—"

The man in black turned his twisted smile on her. "The fault is mine, dear lady. I believe I recognize your voice. Do I have the pleasure of addressing Miss Ermina Ferrington?"

Miss Ferrington blinked and poked her fingers at her hair. "Er—why, yes. I am she."

"I thought so. We have conversed by telephone. It is a great honor to meet you in person. I am Mattheus

Mergal, of Boston. And you are exactly as charming as your voice sounded."

One of the high-school boys snorted and turned away. His shoulders shook as he tried to look interested in the door frame, but Miss Ferrington didn't notice. She extended her hand. "I am pleased to meet you," she said in a soft voice.

Mr. Mergal took her hand and inclined his head over it. He slowly raised his eyes until his gaze locked on hers. "I am sure that you will forgive the young man's honest mistake," he said.

"Why, yes, of course. Er, Johnny, you had better run downstairs and—and do whatever it is that you should be doing."

Johnny hurried away, glad to escape. A few minutes later he saw Mergal pass through the Colonial Life Room and into the foyer. In another second the door opened and closed as he left the museum. Johnny followed and opened the front door just wide enough to peek outside. The black-clad figure strode along in the afternoon sunlight. Across West Merrimack Street from the museum were the gates of Haggstrum College, brick pillars crowned with concrete lions. Mergal crossed the street and walked through the gates and up the drive to an old black Plymouth parked in the shade of an aspen. Without glancing behind him, he climbed into the car, and a moment later it chugged away, leaving a very troubled Johnny Dixon wondering just who the threatening Mr. Mergal was.

CHAPTER THREE

As soon as Johnny got home, he went to see Professor Childermass. At the mention of the strange man, the professor's face grew red. "Mattheus Mergal, of Boston!" he growled. "A crackpot if there ever was one!"

"Do you know him?" asked Johnny.

"I've never actually met him, but he has telephoned me three or four times this summer, trying to buy the Blackleach collection from me. I won't sell the stuff— not because I hate to part with it, but just because I refuse to be pestered into anything! Well, John, if that unsavory character turns up again, you have my permission to tell him to pay me a visit. *I* will send him on his way with a flea in his ear! Now come into the kitchen and tell me what you think of a little experiment of mine.

It's a double-fudge mocha mousse, and I suspect it is just the thing for a warm June afternoon."

The dessert was cool and gloppy and delicious, but despite Johnny's hints, Professor Childermass gave no sign of wanting to discuss the mysterious Mr. Mergal. At last Johnny crossed the street to his own house. He watched television for a while. Then he read a science-fiction novel about a high-school boy in the twenty-first century, who is rocketed to a strange planet. The earth is so crowded with people that there is no room for him and the other teenagers.

At seven Gramma called Johnny to dinner, and after the meal he and Grampa played a couple of games of checkers as they listened to a Red Sox–Detroit Tigers game on the radio. The Red Sox lost—as happened all too frequently—and by the time Johnny went to bed, he had almost forgotten the strange incident in the Gudge Museum.

The next morning the professor was off somewhere, and Johnny had no chores to do, so he went downtown. There were a few kids in Peter's Sweet Shop on Merrimack Street, but he didn't know them. He had a soda and then wandered out, feeling sorry for himself. If only Fergie were here, Johnny thought, we'd go for a long walk and talk about all sorts of crazy stuff. Strolling around Duston Heights alone wasn't nearly as much fun.

Still, Johnny had nothing else to do. He walked aimlessly and wound up at the athletic field, where a raucous game of baseball was going on. No use in trying to join in—a couple of tough kids from St. Michael's School were playing, and they didn't think much of Johnny's abilities. He noticed another lonely figure, a kid in a baggy white T-shirt, a red baseball cap, and blue jeans, standing ahead of him and staring at the game. The kid leaned on a bat that had its handle thrust through the strap of a fielder's mitt. Another rotten player, Johnny decided. Feeling left out, he turned and started to plod away.

"Hey, kid! Wanna play flies and grounders?"

Johnny turned around, surprised. He had assumed the youngster with the bat and glove was a boy, but the voice was a girl's. She was tall and skinny, with a pug nose and a spatter of freckles across her cheeks. "Uh, sure," Johnny said hesitantly.

"C'mon. Their Highnesses won't let me play, but they can't stop us from hittin' a few. Is there someplace good to practice?"

"The park," Johnny said. "It's not far from here."

They walked east on Merrimack Street, then cut over to Round Pond. A semicircle of small ponds lay on this side of town, and a grassy park offered lots of open space. A few people were eating picnic lunches up under the trees, but Johnny and the girl found a nice, level stretch of grass. "Uh, I'm not very good," Johnny confessed. "They won't let me play either."

" 'S okay," returned the girl with a grin. "You don't hafta be Dom DiMaggio to play flies and grounders! By the way, my name's Sarah Channing."

"I'm Johnny Dixon."

Sarah nodded. "We've just moved here," she said. "My dad's gonna teach at Haggstrum College in the fall."

Johnny's face brightened. "Yeah? I know a history teacher there. Professor Childermass. He lives across the street from me."

"Dad teaches English," said Sarah. "Wanna bat first or field first?"

They played for an hour or so, and then Sarah said, "Let me see something. I'm gonna pitch a few to you, nothing tricky. Take a good cut at them." She pushed her red cap up on her forehead, went into a windup, and pitched a clean strike. Johnny missed it, grunted in irritation, and then trotted to retrieve the ball. He tossed it back, and she said, "Again."

Johnny swung and missed three times, a humiliating strikeout. Sarah came over to him and said, "Get into your stance again."

Raising the bat, Johnny crouched a bit. "Choke up on the bat a little. That's good, now hold still," Sarah said. He felt her grab the end of the bat and move it away from his shoulder. "Now keep it right there." She nudged his feet a little farther apart. "Don't bend your knees so much. Get your chin up." She inspected him as if he were a sculpture she had been working on. "That's better. I'm gonna pitch you a pretty easy one. When you swing, try really hard to keep your shoulders level. Keep your eye on the ball, and don't blink when you swing. Keep your elbows pretty loose, but keep control of the bat. Ready?"

"I guess so," said Johnny, without much hope.

"Here we go." She wound up and tossed him a beauty. Johnny squinted, swung, and connected with a solid *thonk!* To his surprise, the ball sprang away in a sizzling drive.

"It's a hot line drive down the third-base line!" whooped Sarah. "Dixon got a piece of that one, folks! It's a base hit for Johnny Dixon, who some folks say is the next Dom DiMaggio!"

Johnny was blushing furiously. "You took it easy on me," he said.

Sarah chased the ball down and trotted back, grinning. "Sure I did," she yelled. "But the next one's gonna be a little harder. Ready, Ace?"

Every once in a while Sarah interrupted her pitching to come over and criticize Johnny's stance. He made the adjustments she recommended, and before long he was hitting one out of four even when she was pitching fastballs and curves. "Not so bad," she said when they both got tired. "I figure you at a batting average of about .250. Betcha you could boost that with a little practice."

Johnny could not help grinning. He and Fergie played all the time, but Fergie—who was a great natural athlete—was not much of a coach and had never offered him this kind of help. Just wait, Johnny thought. Fergie's in for a surprise next time we play!

He and Sarah switched places, and Sarah made quite

a few nice hits. "Boy," Johnny said, loping back after having retrieved a long one, "I don't see why those guys won't let *you* play. You're good!"

" 'Cause I'm a *gir*-ul," Sarah returned, making a face. "And 'cause they don't know how good I am. It's rough being the new kid in town. Hey, that's enough. It's hot and I'm getting tired."

"You thirsty?" Johnny asked, taking his glove off and walking over to where she leaned on the bat.

"Yeah," admitted Sarah. "Parched."

"Uh, you want to go to Peter's Sweet Shop for a soda or something?"

"Are you just feeling sorry for me?" demanded Sarah, scowling fiercely.

Johnny felt his face turn red. "I—I didn't mean—"

After a moment Sarah smiled—a surprisingly shy smile. "That's okay. I thought you were kidding me. I'd love to have a soda, but I'll buy my own, okay?" She took her cap off and ran her fingers through her hair. It was red and cut very short. "You can tell me all about this place on the way. We just moved in, and I feel like a fish out of water. Say, do you know St. Michael's School?"

"Yeah," Johnny said, surprised. "I go there."

"Really? I'm going there too! Listen, are the sisters big on walloping your hands with a ruler?"

"No," Johnny said. "Hardly any of them do that."

"That's a relief. I was in a Catholic girls' school out

in Minnesota, and those nuns had arms on them like Babe Ruth."

They chatted together as they walked to the ice-cream shop and discovered that they would be in the same grade. Johnny was delighted. Sarah was a little imposing as a friend—she had that air of taking charge—but she had a super sense of humor. And just like him, she had always had some trouble fitting in. She had been miserable at her last school, she told him. When the other girls went ga-ga over singers like Eddie Fisher, she memorized baseball statistics. "Lots of other girls made fun of me," she confessed over a vanilla soda. "Just because I don't like dancing and dresses and moonlit walks, and I do like baseball and cars and horses."

Johnny shrugged. Whatever Sarah liked was fine with him. "I'm terrible at sports," he admitted. "But I'm good at English, Latin, and history, and pretty good at science and math. I guess I don't make friends very easily either."

"Let's be friends, then," said Sarah. "You need a friend because you're lonely, and I need one because I'm a stranger in a strange land. Deal?"

"Deal." They locked pinkies on it, a ritual Johnny had never heard of before. For a few minutes they sipped their sodas. Then Johnny said, "I've got a summer job in the museum across the street from the college."

"Huh," said Sarah. "Must be boring."

Thinking of the Sophonsoba Peabody Room, Johnny

nodded. "Sometimes it is. But there's a Witch Room, and that's kind of interesting. You know about the Salem witch trials, don't you?"

She did not. Johnny happily explained about them, and then told her about the witch hysteria in Duston Heights for good measure. "Huh," she said. "I guess people were pretty stupid in the olden days."

Johnny sighed, stirring the foamy dregs of his soda with his straw. He happened to know that not everyone who believed in witches and magic was stupid. In fact, he had been through some pretty harrowing adventures with the professor and Fergie—adventures that sometimes threatened to turn nasty and that had even involved diabolical magic. But he knew that most people were like Sarah: In their opinion, anyone who thought ghosts and witches and magic were real had to have a screw loose. He almost told Sarah some of the things that had happened to him, but he thought better of it. They finished their sodas and went outside. As they sauntered along the street, Sarah asked, "So what does your dad do?"

"He's a pilot in the Air Force," replied Johnny.

"Wow! No kidding? That's great!"

"Yeah," Johnny said. "I guess."

"What's wrong?"

Johnny made a face. "Well, I don't get to see him all that often. My mom died a few years ago—"

"I'm sorry," Sarah said.

"Thanks. And Dad was flying a fighter plane in Korea, so I came here to live with my grandparents."

Sarah stopped and gave him a sharp look. "Wait a minute. Was he that guy who got shot down and then escaped back to American lines?"

"Yes," said Johnny. "Major Harrison Dixon. But he was a captain then."

"I read about him in *Life*! Your dad's a hero! Boy, *my* dad never does anything more exciting than grade an essay. You're lucky, Dixon!"

"I suppose."

"So what's wrong?"

They began to walk again. Johnny said, "The problem is that usually I see Dad for just a few weeks every year. During Christmas vacation this year we're going to go deep-sea fishing in Florida."

"Great! Can I meet him when he comes?"

"Sure."

"Suppose he'd give me his autograph?"

Johnny looked hard at her, but she didn't seem to be teasing him. "Sure, he would," he told her. "But he's just Dad. I mean, he doesn't think of himself as a hero."

Sarah shrugged, and for a few steps she was silent. Then she spoke up again: "Goin' to Florida, huh? You know, the only time I've ever seen the ocean was when we flew into Boston? It sure doesn't look like much through an airplane window."

Looking at a marquee ahead of them, Johnny noticed

the theater was showing a Saturday matinee. It was a film he had seen before, *Captain Horatio Hornblower*. He asked, "Hey, want to see the movie?"

"That's a silly title," said Sarah. "Who is he, Clarabelle's brother?" Clarabelle Hornblower was a clown on *The Howdy Doody Show*, a puppet show that came on TV every afternoon. It was for little kids.

"No, Captain Hornblower was a sea captain in the British Navy back during the Napoleonic wars," explained Johnny. "See, he's sent on a mission to South America, and then he has to fight a ship that's twice the size of the *Lydia*—that's his ship—and there's this big battle at sea with the two ships firing cannons at each other—"

"Sounds like fun," said Sarah. "Only I'm broke after the sodas."

After a moment's pause Johnny said, "I got paid yesterday. I can buy your ticket. It's not a date or anything. Next time you can buy mine, okay?"

Sarah grinned at him. "You're all right, Dixon. Sure, I guess. Sounds like a pretty good movie."

They went to the show and munched popcorn and guzzled orange sodas as the ship battles, sword fights, and narrow escapes worked themselves out on the screen. When they walked back outside after the movie, the sunlight seemed dazzling and strange. Half a block away, she turned. "Hey, Dixon! What's your phone number?"

He called it out to her. "How about yours?" he asked.

"Don't have one yet. I'll call when we get a phone. Bye!" She put the bat over her shoulder and marched away. Johnny grinned. Maybe, he thought, this wasn't going to be such a terrible summer after all. He strolled back toward Fillmore Street whistling a jaunty tune, with thoughts of the horrible Mr. Mergal, the wizard Esdrias Blackleach, and the mysterious wooden hand very far from his mind.

CHAPTER FOUR

The next day was Sunday. Johnny and his grandparents attended Mass at St. Michael's Church, and there they saw Professor Childermass, whose church attendance was spotty. After the service Professor Childermass and the pastor, Father Thomas Higgins, walked back to the rectory together. Johnny decided to hang around for a while, and his grandparents went home without him.

After a few minutes the priest and the professor came outside again. They made an odd pair. Father Higgins was tall and muscular, with iron-gray hair and a square, grizzled jaw. His dark, bushy eyebrows gave him a constant scowl, but in reality he was a kind, understanding man—and a brave one. He had served in the Army during World War II and had been in the Philippines, where fighting was heavy. And, as Johnny knew, the priest had also faced some wicked and dangerous supernatural foes, including ghosts, sorcerers, and zombies. Now he was deep in conversation with the professor. Johnny hesitated to interrupt, but Professor Childermass noticed him, gave a slight start, and beckoned him over. Johnny joined them at the corner of the church.

"Hello, Johnny," Father Higgins said. "Roderick here was just telling me about your unpleasant visitor, Mr. Mergal."

"And about Esdrias Blackleach," added the professor. "In fact, I was asking Higgy if he would bless that wretched relic of a hand. Ever since I showed it to you, I've been having nasty dreams about it." The professor gave a little shiver. "In my dreams I imagine that it's come to life and is dragging itself around by the fingers. It cree-ee-eeps up my bedclothes, cra-a-awls to my pillow, and clutches me by the throat!" Professor Childermass put a hand to his throat and coughed. "I wake up choking, jump out of bed, and discover that the sinister statuette is locked exactly where I left it."

"I told him to use it for kindling," said Father Higgins.

"Hang it, Higgy," returned the professor, "it's almost three hundred years old! I couldn't call myself a historian and run around burning up antiques like that."

"Are you going to bless the hand, Father?" asked Johnny.

Father Higgins shrugged. "I suppose. Although I'm

tempted to let it remain unblessed, if it's really needling Roderick's conscience. At least it got him to Mass, which is more than I've managed to do for a month!"

"Come over this afternoon, then," said Professor Childermass. "I'll expect you around three."

"Can I come too, Professor?" asked Johnny. "After all, this whole thing started because of me."

Professor Childermass smiled. He liked Johnny Dixon immensely, because he felt that the lonely, brainy, timid young man was a great deal like he himself had been as a boy. "I don't see why not," he said. "Come on over, and we'll deal with the wizard's handiwork together."

Johnny walked home, enjoying the warm sunshine and the bright, clear sky. But when he turned onto Fillmore Street, his heart thudded suddenly. A black-and-white police car was parked in front of his house! What terrible thing had happened? Johnny broke into a frantic run. He pounded across the front porch, opened the door, and found Gramma, Grampa, and two policemen standing in the parlor. They looked up in surprise.

"Uh—I saw the police car," Johnny gasped. "What's wrong?"

"Nothin' here, Johnny," Gramma said. "Land sakes! You're white as a sheet. Don't worry—we're all right."

Grampa Dixon, a tall, stoop-shouldered old man with a wrinkled face and a bald, freckled head, made a tutting noise with his tongue. "Burglars, Johnny! Right here on Fillmore Street! Did you ever hear the likes of that in your life? Right in broad daylight, an' on Sunday too!"

Johnny had interrupted the story. He stood and listened to the rest of it, piecing together what must have happened. Gramma and Grampa had strolled home from Mass. As they neared their house, Gramma noticed something odd across the street. The professor was not back, because his garage door was open and his maroon Pontiac was not inside, yet a light burned in his study, on the second floor of his house. As she watched, that light went out—but then a light came on in the room next door. Grampa had wanted to go over and see who was in there, but Gramma had insisted that they call the police.

A few minutes before the police car arrived, a man wearing a long black raincoat and a black hat pulled low over his face had come out of the professor's house and had hurried away. Grampa tried to follow him, but his arthritis kept him from walking very fast, and the man disappeared around the corner of the next street. By the time Grampa got back, the police had arrived, and then Johnny showed up.

Johnny looked out the bay window just then and saw the professor driving up. The two policemen hurried across the street as the old man was putting his car away, and then the three went inside the professor's house. Gramma put a protective hand on Johnny's shoulder. "Folks are gettin' awfully low," she said in a hurt voice. "Imagine! Hardly anybody in Duston Heights ever locks their door at night, but from now on I guess we better start checkin' to make sure ours is locked."

"What did the man look like, Grampa?" Johnny asked.

His grandfather sighed. "Like a big black ghost," he said. "With his raincoat collar turned up an' that big, floppy-brimmed hat, like th' Shadow used to wear on the covers of his books, he didn't give me a good look at his face. But he moved mighty fast, that's for sure."

The Dixons had a troubled lunch. Gramma made tomato-vegetable soup, and Grampa made tall roast beef sandwiches, piling slices of homemade sourdough bread with beef, tomatoes, onions, and lettuce. The food was hearty, but no one talked much, and after they had finished, Johnny was glad to see the police pulling away from the curb. "I'm going over to see the professor," he called, and ran out the door.

Professor Childermass, his face as dark as a thundercloud, was standing in his front doorway. "Hello," he growled as Johnny hurried over. "Welcome to Castle Childermass, the victim of a human earthquake!"

Once inside, Johnny saw what the professor meant. Everything was turned upside down. The sofa in the living room had been cut to shreds, with wads of stuffing erupting through long slashes. Books had been tumbled off shelves; the hall closet had been ransacked, with overcoats and fedoras and galoshes strewn everywhere. The kitchen was a wreck. Plates had been strewn around and broken, the oven was open, the refrigerator emptied. Bottles of Tabasco sauce, ketchup, and milk had been thrown carelessly down, breaking and spilling. Lettuce and tomatoes lay squashed and trodden on the floor. Part of a baked chicken had been tossed into a corner, and other food lay here and there. Johnny swallowed. "Professor, did—did he get the—"

"No," Professor Childermass said shortly. "The precious Mr. Mergal did *not* find the hand."

Johnny blinked. "Gosh, Professor, do you think it was really him?"

"Who else?" The professor lit one of his Balkan Sobranie cigarettes. "Of course, I will bet you dollars to doughnuts that the man has a perfect alibi. And no one except your grandparents seems to have noticed the villain. Oh, I *wish* I had been at home when he came calling! I—I—" the professor spluttered as words failed him. He grabbed a plate from a heap jumbled on the white enameled table and smashed it on the floor. Then he hurled a saucer. He offered one to Johnny. "Care to try your luck?"

Johnny shook his head. "N-no, sir."

"It doesn't help, anyway." He placed the saucer on the table. "I am going to have to refurnish my house from scratch! Oh, that misbegotten miscreant will pay for this, mark my words!"

The doorbell rang, making them both jump. It was Father Higgins. When he came into the house, he stared around with wide, wondering eyes. Brusquely, Professor Childermass explained what had happened. He told

Johnny and the priest to go up to his study. "The hound did less damage there than elsewhere," the professor observed. "I'll join you in a couple of shakes."

When he and Father Higgins entered the study, Johnny saw what the professor meant. True, all the books had been tumbled out of the shelves and the shelves themselves, made of bricks and boards, had been knocked apart. The stuffed owl had even been thrown off its round stand, and every drawer in the professor's desk had been pulled out and dumped on the floor. Still, since the study was never very tidy anyway, it didn't look all that bad.

The professor came in, shaking his head and gripping the wooden hand. "Here's the Cracker Jack prize that caused all this, Higgy. Take a whack at it, and see what holy water and holy words can do!"

Father Higgins set the carved hand on the desk, sprinkled it with holy water, and recited a prayer of blessing. Nothing happened. "There," said the priest with a sigh. "I don't know if we've accomplished anything, Rod, but maybe that will keep this nasty little creepy-crawler out of your nightmares. Now, I don't have anything much to do until evening Mass, so if you want, I'll help pick up this place a little."

Johnny joined in, and after a couple of hours, they had the downstairs rooms in fairly decent condition. The professor sighed over his kitchen. Baking was his favorite hobby, and although his cake pans, saucepans, and other cooking utensils were intact, he had hardly a cup, saucer, or plate to his name. They piled broken crockery into a big, battered old ash can. "The police told me to give them a list of anything that is missing," he growled. "I can't see that anything has been stolen, but I'm missing all of my dishes, my easy chair and sofa, and about half of my self-respect! I plan to be prepared if my visitor comes calling again."

"You take it easy," warned Father Higgins. "You're no longer the spry boy who charged a machine-gun nest single-handedly at the battle of the Argonne Forest."

The professor's eyes glittered behind his spectacles. "No, but by heaven, I'm man enough to make a midnight marauder know he's been in a fight if he tangles with me! I think tomorrow I'll shop for furniture, then drive up to Durham, New Hampshire. My old friend Charley Coote may have some advice on how to deal with that dratted wooden carving." Dr. Charles Coote was a specialist in the folklore of magic and sorcery, and he taught at the University of New Hampshire. Johnny knew and liked the old man, and he almost asked if he could go along—but then he remembered he would have to report to the museum. Having a summer job had some drawbacks.

That evening Professor Childermass had dinner with the Dixons. Over pot roast and mashed potatoes, the professor pretended to shrug off the burglary. He said it was probably just some homeless tramp looking for money kept in a sock or stuffed under a mattress. He kept telling Henry and Kate Dixon not to worry. "I've been thinking of redecorating for some time," he finished with a chuckle. "This just hurries me along a little, that's all."

Johnny saw Grampa and Gramma exchange a worried look. They knew their bristly, foul-tempered neighbor very well, and they knew he was not acting like himself. But when Grampa suggested that he might want to stay in the guest bedroom that night, the professor just shook his head. "Thank you, Henry, but I prefer my own little bed, rumpled and tossed though it may be. I shall be quite safe. My doors will be firmly locked, and I plan to have Brown Bess standing guard right at the head of my bed!"

Later, when the professor had returned home, Johnny asked Grampa Dixon who Brown Bess was. The old man shook his head. "Well, Johnny, that's a kind o' nickname. Years ago th' professor used to do some huntin', before he decided that killing animals was cruel if you weren't gonna eat the meat. But he still has his huntin' rifle, a nifty World War I surplus Enfield. It's the same weapon he used t' carry in th' Army. Because it was made in England, he used t' call it Brown Bess, the same name the British gave to their muskets durin' the American Revolution."

Johnny swallowed. He did not know what kind of shot his old friend was, but he hoped there would be no opportunity for the professor to have to fire Brown Bess.

CHAPTER FIVE

Monday morning passed with no news from Professor Childermass. Johnny finished his work at one o'clock, as usual, and as he left the museum, he was surprised to see Sarah Channing on the sidewalk outside. "Hi," she said with a grin. She was wearing jeans, sneakers, and a vastly oversized University of Minnesota football jersey. "So can I tour the museum, or what?"

"Sure," said Johnny. "Only we'll have to do it right now, because the museum closes at two on Mondays and Wednesdays. Is that why you're here?"

"Nope," returned Sarah. "Been helping my dad move books into his new office. He's shelving them now, so my job's done. I'm just the pack animal."

A few other people milled about in the museum, but

not many. Johnny showed Sarah the Sophonsoba Pea-body Room, the Colonial Life Room, and the other ex-hibits on the first and second floors. Last of all they went upstairs to the Curiosities Room. Sarah didn't seem very impressed by the displays there. They went downstairs together. "Oh, by the way," said Sarah, "we're getting our phone today. The phone man was there when Dad and I packed the station wagon this morning. I'll call you tonight, okay?"

"Sure," Johnny replied. Sarah said she had to go see if her dad had finished, and she waved good-bye as she crossed the street. Johnny got on his bike, but before he pushed off from the curb, Miss Ferrington's sharp voice called his name. He got off his bike, surprised. "Yes, Miss Ferrington?"

The stern-faced curator sniffed. "I have a small job for you, if you want to earn a little overtime pay."

"Sure. I mean, yes, I would. I'll put this away." Johnny rolled his bike around to the bike stand beside the build-ing. Then he returned to the front of the museum, where Miss Ferrington waited for him. "What is it?" he asked, going back up the steps.

Miss Ferrington glanced at her wristwatch. "The de-livery service is dropping off a carton of cleaning sup-plies. They will have to be unpacked and stored. I must go to a meeting of the Duston Heights Historical So-ciety, so I cannot remain here. I'll want you to open the loading door, sign for the carton, and then put the sup-plies away. Can you do that?"

"Yes, Miss Ferrington," replied Johnny.

Miss Ferrington gave him a small key ring with just three keys on it. "This one unlocks the loading door. This one unlocks my office. After you finish, put the keys on my desk. I'll leave my office door and the front door set to lock when you close them. Put a note on my desk telling me how late you have to stay, and I'll add that much to your pay on Friday."

It didn't sound hard. Miss Ferrington left, and at first the empty museum seemed spooky. Johnny kept hearing creaks and faint groans, but they were just the sounds of the old house settling. He wished he had a radio to keep him company, but the best he could do was to round up a few old copies of *Yankee* magazine. He leafed through these, growing more and more nervous.

Finally, at about two-fifty, he heard the buzzer that was connected to the rear loading door. He hurried to unlock it. A man waited there with a clipboard and a big cardboard carton. "Hi, Captain," said the man, who wore the khaki uniform of a delivery company. "You want to sign for this stuff?"

Johnny signed the receipt and carried the carton inside. He unpacked all the items it contained—sweeping compound, toilet paper, furniture polish, window cleaner, and other supplies. He put most of the supplies on the shelves of the janitor's closet on the first floor, but he took a gallon jug of liquid soap around to fill up all the dispensers in the rest rooms. He checked his watch. It was four minutes after three. He left a note on

Miss Ferrington's desk, placed the key ring on top of it, and carefully closed both her office door and the front door as he left.

He rode his bike home and had a sandwich. Then he crossed the street to see if the professor was home, but the old man had not returned from his trip to Durham. Later that afternoon the professor reappeared, but a furniture van pulled up just as he drove into his garage, and the professor had to supervise the unloading. He didn't have time to talk to Johnny. Not long after the van departed, the professor drove away again, and he had not returned by the time Sarah called at eight that evening.

At the museum the next day the time seemed to crawl. When Johnny returned home from work, the professor was still away. Feeling lonely and tired, Johnny raided the refrigerator, picked up *Ben-Hur*, a book about ancient Rome that he was reading, and went to sit on the front porch glider. He read and munched Ritz crackers spread with pimiento-flavored cream cheese. The copy of *Ben-Hur* was old, and its spotted pages smelled a little musty, but that helped pull Johnny back into the days of harsh slavery and exciting chariot races. The day was hot and still, and before long, Johnny nodded. He fell asleep sitting there, hunched over and breathing softly. As he dozed, he dreamed of men in black robes and terrified women who stood before them to be judged for witch-craft.

A hateful face loomed over it all. A thin, gaunt, evil face. It looked almost like someone Johnny knew, but not quite. It reminded him of Mr. Mergal, but there was something different too—

In his dream Johnny saw the pale lips of the face move. "John Michael Dixon!" a gravelly voice rumbled. "Thou hast been accused of the vile and ungodly crime of witchcraft! How dost thou plead?"

Johnny woke with a start—and yelped in alarm! From just outside the screen door, a face *was* staring right at him!

"For heaven's sake," grumbled Professor Childermass in his crabbiest voice as he opened the door and stepped onto the porch. "Have I turned blue and red and purple, like a mandrill? What's wrong with you, John?"

Johnny sat up, feeling dizzy. "Sorry, Professor," he gasped. "I guess I was having a bad dream, and then you showed up, and when I saw you watching me, I thought it was part of the dream."

"Oh, peachy," growled the professor. "Now I'm a nightmare. Soon people will be hiring me to haunt houses. Well, I'm sorry I gave you the galloping woo-hoos, but I want to talk to you. Are you busy?"

Johnny shook his head.

"Then come with me. For the last couple of days I've been conferring with Charley Coote about that little goodie the burglar was looking for, and I want to bring you up-to-date."

Johnny followed the professor across the street and up to his study, which was more or less back in shape. The professor settled into the chair behind his desk, and

Johnny sat in a big, bristly armchair. It was new and smelled funny, a little like starch and a little like furniture polish. Professor Childermass frowned and said, "Well, to begin way back at the beginning, all the troubles seemed to spring from Esdrias Blackleach. According to Charley, Blackleach was even worse than I thought."

"He was a real magician, wasn't he?" asked Johnny. "And he did something awful with that wooden hand!"

Professor Childermass sighed. "Don't tell me your imagination's been working overtime about that miserable hand, John. Esdrias went to his reward one stormy August first more than two hundred and sixty years ago. I hardly think he's anyone to worry about."

"But that Mergal man from Boston is looking for his stuff. And I *know* I felt that hand move," said Johnny, sounding miserable.

"We won't argue," said the professor, giving him a sympathetic look. He drummed his fingers on the desk. "Let me tell you what Charley learned. It is Dr. Coote's belief that Esdrias Blackleach really and truly thought of himself as a wizard. There's nothing written that absolutely confirms that, but from old diaries and journals left behind by Blackleach's contemporaries, Charley thinks it's so. More, Charley is certain that Mr. Esdrias Blackleach was in truth the *only* certified, bonafide, guaranteed, accept-no-substitutes *practicing* wizard anywhere in Massachusetts back in 1692."

"I just knew it," said Johnny. "What did he do, Professor?"

"Charley and I can only speculate. I don't know where Esdrias Blackleach found his power. It may have come from the devil himself, for all I know. Certainly, over the years his enemies had a curious series of misfortunes. What do you know of the Salem witchcraft mania, John?"

Johnny shrugged. "Just what I've read in history books."

"Let me summarize. In 1692, down in Salem Village, the Reverend Samuel Parris, with whom Blackleach had quarreled, discovered the witch persecution in his own house. As the weeks went by, a number of hysterical girls accused more and more people of witchcraft. Before autumn the good people of Salem Village had accused more than a hundred people of witchcraft. The madness spread to other towns, like Gloucester, Beverly, Haverhill, and our very own Duston Heights. It was a funny thing about the accusations. They ruined homes, destroyed lives, and wrecked families, and yet they seemed to make Esdrias Blackleach a wealthy man."

"How?" asked Johnny.

"Well, being accused of witchcraft made people eager to leave Massachusetts. Every time someone left the colony, or even worse, went to the gallows, old Esdrias Blackleach got a little richer. He acquired all their property—land, usually, but often cattle or personal goods—at ridiculously low prices. And no one ever named *him* as a suspected warlock."

"But he was?"

Professor Childermass nodded and sighed. "In my opinion and Charley's, he did work evil magic—of a kind," he said at length. "I don't know if you could call what he did *sorcery* in any real sense. I *don't* believe he hexed pigs and goats and cows, or caused milk to sour, or raised thunderstorms, or any of that nonsense. However, I *do* think that he did wickedness enough by convincing others that people like Goody Cory or Rebecca Nurse or Reverend Burroughs were tormenting them. So the unfortunate, innocent victims went to the noose— and Blackleach went free."

"Oh," said Johnny, a little let down. "Just that kind of magic."

The professor shook his head. "Don't discount the wicked power of gossip and hatred, John, and don't be fooled into believing that words cannot harm you. People who think that magic works, as the Salem villagers did, find that it really *does* work. A hex spell kills its victim precisely because the victim believes in the spell. Now, with a really clever person, as Blackleach assuredly was, and a credulous group who already believe in witchcraft, all sorts of 'supernatural' things can happen. Or at least, people will all swear that they happened, which amounts to the same thing."

"But does any of this help you?"

"Knowledge always helps, John. Now Charley is

tracking down a crumbly old manuscript that is supposed to be a first-hand account of Blackleach's deviltry. That may tell us more. Until then I'll stand on what I know about the old reprobate: He was a sour, vicious, evil-tempered villain who wished the world nothing but ill."

"What about Mr. Mergal?" asked Johnny somewhat timidly.

The professor glared. "Oh, that scoundrel! I told the police to check him out, and he has an ironclad alibi. He lives in a hotel in Boston, and according to the manager, Mr. Mergal was having lunch in his room about the time my house was burgled. The police reached him at his hotel address. You see, he's doing research in the libraries down there. He admitted going to the Gudge Museum, but he says he was just looking at the possessions that Blackleach used to own to get in the proper spirit to write about the man. Ha! I can spot a phony a mile away. Whatever our precious Mr. Mergal may be, he is definitely *not* a historian. Trust me, John, you know more about the Colonial period than that blasted blowhard does."

Johnny shifted uncomfortably in his armchair. "I'm worried," he said. "Mr. Mergal didn't act sane, Professor. He was, well, spooky."

Professor Childermass' face glowed a malignant, magnificent red, and his muttonchops bristled alarmingly. "I have yet to encounter a foe as formidable as I," he said with menacing softness. "If that man puts one foot on Fillmore Street, I shall deal with him. As for the late unlamented Mr. Esdrias Blackleach, he passed away nearly three hundred years ago—" the professor broke off, a strange expression coming over his face. "Odd," he murmured. "I never thought of that before. Most odd."

"What?" Johnny asked, far from reassured.

"Blackleach's death," muttered Professor Childermass. "According to Charley's books, he died at twelve midnight during a freakish, terrible thunderstorm on a summer night in 1692. The date was August first."

Johnny felt goosebumps marching up his arms. "Lammas."

The professor's eyes glittered, and he nodded. "You've read about such things too, I see. Yes, Lammas. One of the four high Sabbats, or feast days, of the witches. A fitting night for the devil to claim his own. Or perhaps just a cosmic joke." The professor gave a wry grin, but his tone sounded serious—very, very serious, indeed.

CHAPTER SIX

For a couple of weeks Johnny heard no more news of either the wizard Blackleach or the sinister Mr. Mergal. June ended and July came in with hot days and muggy, warm nights. More and more, Miss Ferrington relied on Johnny to do little things at the museum. She hated to be there on Monday afternoons, when deliveries came, and Johnny always had the little extra job of waiting in the echoing, deserted museum for an hour or two. He would unlock the back door, store the supplies away, and leave the key on Miss Ferrington's desk before leaving. He always remembered to check the front door, which locked behind him, and he never had any trouble.

Johnny introduced Professor Childermass to Sarah, with a little fear and trembling. The professor could be rude and scary when he was upset or preoccupied, although Johnny knew he had a warm heart. He need not have worried, because the professor could also be a real charmer when he chose. The old man was delighted to make Sarah's acquaintance, especially when she agreed with him that the Red Sox didn't deserve their fourth-place standing but had suffered from a run of bad umpires. In turn, Sarah liked Professor Childermass because he didn't treat her like a child, but listened to her opinions as if they really mattered. The three of them didn't go to movies or gorge on hot-fudge sundaes the way Johnny, Fergie, and the professor did, but their talks were cordial and interesting.

Independence Day was a holiday for Johnny. At first it didn't seem as if the day would be very exciting. Gramma and Grampa were planning to drive over to Lowell on the Fourth to visit Gramma's sister Martha. She was younger than Gramma, and she had a house full of antiques and a deep distrust of young, active boys. Whenever Johnny was there, Great-aunt Martha made him sit very still in an armchair the whole time, so he wouldn't break any of her precious keepsakes. It wasn't much fun.

So Johnny was glad when the professor invited him and Sarah to a cookout instead. Normally Professor Childermass asked his friends over to his weedy, overgrown backyard for hot dogs and hamburgers once or twice a year. This time, however, he suggested that it might be nice instead to picnic in the park on the east side of Duston Heights. The trip to the park would be a bit of an expedition, but the professor's terrific hamburgers would make the effort worthwhile. He added his own secret ingredients to the ground beef, then cooked the burgers over a charcoal fire that had to be just right. The results were always juicy and delicious.

On Monday morning, which was the Fourth, the professor packed everything in his maroon Pontiac, and he, Johnny, and Sarah left for the park in a cloud of exhaust smoke. They arrived early enough to claim one of the stone grills and a picnic table on the shady side of the park. The professor insisted that he needed privacy to prepare the charcoal and begin the hamburgers, so he ordered Johnny and Sarah to find something to occupy them.

Sarah had brought her bat, ball, and glove, and Johnny had a floppy old fielder's glove that had once belonged to his dad. They planned to play flies and grounders, but a bunch of boys were playing baseball, so Johnny and Sarah walked over to see if they could join in. Some of the kids in town were beginning to realize that Sarah was no slouch as a baseball player.

They were in luck—sort of. Tim Jacobs was the captain of the team in the field, and as soon as he saw them, he yelled, "We get Sarah!"

Unfortunately their luck ran out with that, because the leader of the team at bat was Eddie Tompke, a boy who had made Johnny's life miserable at every Boy Scout meeting. Eddie was a muscular, handsome kid, but he had a long-standing grudge against Johnny. Until the previous year, they had been in the same class at school, but Eddie wasn't a very good student and had been left back. He pretended that it didn't bother him, but he always pestered Johnny, calling him a brownnose and a teacher's pet and playing all sorts of mean tricks on him at Scout meetings.

Eddie scowled and yelled, "No way you get her, if we gotta take Four-Eyes. So the girl can't play."

"Hey, we'll take him too," Tim said. "That'll give us eight players on a side, so it's fair. Sarah, you take shortstop. Uh, Johnny, you play right field, okay?"

Johnny knew very well that right field was where they stuck you when you weren't any good. He tugged the tattered fielder's glove on and trotted out to right field, his head down and his mind full of worries. Would he foul up and make a costly error? What would happen if a high fly smacked him in the face, broke his glasses, and sent sharp pieces of glass into his eyes? He might be permanently blinded.

But when he turned, Sarah gave him a cheerful wave, and he returned it. "Might as well go down swinging," he muttered, hoping he could get through the game without disgracing himself.

Sarah took her position as shortstop and crouched over. Tim was pitching. They tossed the ball around the infield and then they settled down to the game. The first batter was tall and solid and looked as if he could hit.

But Tim's fastball was singing, and after two pitches, the count was o and 2.

Tim studied the batter for a moment, and then he wound up and threw his famous curve. It broke exactly right, and the batter swung around like a gate, cleanly missing the ball. "Three strikes and you're out of there!" crowed Pete Freeling, the catcher, tossing the ball back to Tim. "One down, two to go. Attaboy, Timmy!"

The game was fun. After five innings Eddie's team was ahead five to three. Johnny had batted twice. The first time he popped up a foul that Eddie caught, and the second time he went down swinging, but that was no disgrace. Many on both teams had done the same. In fact, in the top of the sixth Tim easily struck out the first two batters.

Next at bat was a scowling Eddie Tompke. He pounded his bat on the plate. Tim tried an outside pitch, but Tompke just frowned. "Ball one, Timmo," Eddie said with a sneer. "Ya gonna walk me, ya big fat chicken?"

"C'mon, Tim, he can't hit," Sarah yelled. "Strike him out, baby."

Tim looked mad. Eddie had been yelling insults and laughing at every mistake Tim made. He could really get on a pitcher's nerves. Tim pitched a fastball and Eddie swung. Johnny heard the crack of the bat. For a moment he couldn't even *see* the ball. Then he had it, a blurred streak in the sky. It was going high and far—and it was coming his way.

Johnny backpedaled desperately. The center fielder was hustling over, but he was going to be too late. The ball was already hurtling down. Gritting his teeth, running backward, Johnny threw his gloved hand up. With a stinging slap, the ball smacked into his worn glove.

And stayed there.

The astounding fact that he had caught a high fly ball hit deep to right field practically dazed Johnny. He held the ball up and felt a big goofy grin spread across his face. Pete jumped two feet in the air behind home plate and screamed, "Way to go, my man John! *Yee-ha!*"

It had all happened a lot faster than Johnny thought. Though Eddie was a good base-runner, he was only about halfway to first. He stumbled to a stop, his eyes wide and unbelieving, and when he saw that Johnny really had caught the ball, he cursed and threw his cap on the ground.

"We're up to bat!" Tim yelled, dropping his glove and trotting in. "C'mon, guys, we're two down. Let's get even."

Jimmy King, a tough kid who was a grade ahead of Johnny at St. Michael's, came out to the pitcher's mound, and Johnny tossed the ball to him. Eddie, still standing near first base, sneered at Johnny, "Guess you think you're pretty hot stuff 'cause ya caught one measly ball, huh, Four-Eyes? Just you wait. We're gonna fix you losers good. We're gonna pound you right into the ground."

Sarah tugged Johnny's arm. "Don't pay him any attention," she said, "he just wants to make you mad so you can't hit anything."

"Oh, great," Eddie said. "Get this, guys. Weird Sarah and Johnny Baby are in *lo-ove!* Ya gonna kiss her, Johnny Baby?" Eddie put his hands on his hips, smacking his pursed lips.

"Oh, shut up, Eddie," Johnny said.

"Don't let him get to you," Tim said as Johnny came up to the rest of the team. "That was a good catch, Johnny. Eddie's just mad 'cause usually he's a lot harder to put out. Okay, let's get a couple of runs now."

Eddie played first base. Tim was at bat first, but when he lined a pretty good hit, the left fielder caught it on a bounce and tossed it to Eddie, putting Tim out a step before he reached first. Without any reason for doing it, Eddie slammed the ball against Tim's shoulder. Johnny winced at the sharp sound of the ball thudding into Tim's upper arm. Tim turned, glared at Eddie, and trotted back, massaging his shoulder. "We got 'em," Eddie yelled in derision. "They ain't nothin' but a bun-cha babies and *gir*-uls in *lo-ove!*"

"Darn that Tompke, anyhow," Tim grumbled. "He's gonna pick on the wrong guy someday and get his big fat block knocked off. Go ahead, Sarah. Don't let him make you mad."

Sarah was a switch hitter, and this time she batted left. On the pitcher's mound Jimmy looked a little worried, because Sarah had been in several games by that time, and everyone knew that she was good with a bat. She took two balls before Jimmy tried one in the strike zone. She swung level and fast, and the ball sprang away with a *crack!* It was a whistling line drive to the left of second base, and it hit the ground, bounced, and kept going as two players chased madly after it. Sarah rounded first and pounded into second before the ball came back.

Eddie stomped around on first base and cursed some more.

"Go on, Johnny," Tim said, patting him on the back. "Get us a hit."

Johnny batted right-handed. He pushed his glasses up on his nose, choked up on the bat, and held it away from his shoulder as Sarah had advised, trying hard to stay calm. He was thinking furiously of everything Sarah had taught him. If only he could get a hit—that would be really something. Looking a lot more relaxed now that he was pitching to Johnny, Jimmy threw a fast one, and Johnny swung hard, connecting only with air.

Johnny's heart sank. Who was he kidding? He'd never get a hit off Jimmy, not in a million years. The miserable little blooper he had hit in the second inning was the best he would ever do. Oh, he could occasionally hit them when Sarah pitched, but she was babying him along—

The second pitch streaked in, and this time Johnny tipped it foul. He could feel his face growing hot. Well, he might go down swinging, but at least he could try to do what Sarah had taught him.

He cocked the bat and felt strangely calm as Jimmy

wound up and threw for the third time. The pitch came in fast and a little high, shoulder level, and Johnny knew he had it even before he began his swing. With a solid *thunk!* he connected, sending a bouncing ground ball right to the shortstop. Johnny was already running, knowing it was hopeless.

But the ball took a screwy hop right over the shortstop's glove as Eddie screamed something nasty. The flustered infielder awkwardly scooped the ball up and turned toward third base. That was the right move, but Eddie yelled for the ball. The shortstop looked his way, then back at third base, and then back at Eddie. By the time he made up his mind, Johnny had stepped on first base. Eddie screamed, and the shortstop glowered, but the play stood. Johnny was on first, Sarah on third. It was Johnny's first base-hit ever in a real game. Tim's team was leaping up and down and cheering.

Tim's team was hot. The next kid got a single, but the center fielder quickly scooped up the ball, threw it to second base, and Johnny was out. On the play at second, Sarah scored a run. Johnny trudged back with his head down. "Sorry, guys," he said dismally.

With a laugh, Tim slapped him on the shoulder again. "For what? You put Sarah into position to score, and we got an out left to go. Batter up!"

Their luck held, and the next batter slammed a home run. Paul Deakins struck out, but by then nobody cared, because now the team was ahead by one, and Eddie was almost purple with anger. As the teams changed sides,

Professor Childermass' voice boomed across the park: "Lunch is now served! Mr. Dixon and Miss Channing are to report to the chow line on the double, or I'll throw it all out!"

"Go on," Tim said with a grin. "The way Eddie's screamin' at his guys, I don't think the game's gonna last any longer. Thanks, both of you."

Tim was right. Three of Eddie's players were already walking off in disgust, because Eddie was blaming them for falling behind. The game was going to end with Tim's team up by one, but Eddie got in a parting shot. "Go to the old oddball, you babies!" he yelled. "Next time I catch ya alone, you're in trouble, Dixon! I'm gonna stomp ya!"

Even Eddie's mean-spirited taunts failed to make Johnny feel bad. He grinned at Sarah and shrugged, and she giggled. It was shaping up to be the best day Johnny had seen since Fergie left for Ohio.

If only it could have gone on like that, he would have been very happy.

CHAPTER SEVEN

Johnny, Sarah, and the professor sat at the concrete picnic table and wolfed down the tasty hamburgers. Sarah said they were the best burgers she had ever eaten, and the professor gave her a courtly bow of thanks. Then he brought out a surprise, one of his luscious Sacher tortes, an especially rich, gooey, and delicious chocolate cake. After one bite Sarah moaned, "I think I've died and gone to heaven!"

"My compliments on your discriminating palate," said the professor, beaming. "You are a true gourmet." A crow in a nearby tree cawed, and he grimaced. "Crows are unlovely birds. That one wants a handout, but he can forget it." They had made quite a bit of headway on the cake when Johnny looked to see what had happened on the baseball field. He almost choked.

Standing alone on the diamond was a tall, skinny, bald man dressed in black. His face was gaunt, and from beneath his heavy eyebrows his eyes glowered at them from deep, shadowy sockets.

It was Mattheus Mergal.

Johnny swallowed, reached for his paper cup, and washed the mouthful of cake down with lemonade. "Professor," he gasped. "Look over there!"

"Where?" The professor adjusted his spectacles and stared at the figure in black. "I see nothing more alarming than a gentleman with a dubious sense of style, John. What should I be looking at?"

"It's him," Johnny said. "It's Mr. Mergal, the one from the museum. He's spying on you."

"Indeed? Well, I shall give him something to think about!"

The professor rose, but Johnny was at his side in a second, tugging at his arm. "Oh, gosh, Professor, don't go. He's a terrible person!"

Sarah had heard nothing of Johnny's meeting with Mr. Mergal, and she looked from Johnny to the professor in bewilderment. "Who in heck are you two talking about?" she asked.

"Him," Johnny said, turning and pointing. He blinked, his mouth hanging open in surprise, his trembling finger pointing at an empty park.

Mergal was gone.

It's impossible, Johnny thought, staring at the now-deserted baseball diamond. Only a few beech and white ash trees stood scattered about. Mergal had nowhere to hide, and yet he had completely vanished. "Hmpf," the professor said. "Obviously the man is a coward. Let's forget him and finish our meal like civilized people."

The appearance of the black-clad stranger had cast a pall over the afternoon. The sun grew hazy and bleak. A dry wind began to rattle in the trees, though at ground level it was just a skittish breeze. Johnny felt a chill inside him, and he kept looking around nervously as the three finished their picnic and began to pack the hamper. "That's funny," he said.

"What?" Sarah asked, sounding annoyed.

"Well, there were lots of people here just a few minutes ago. The guys playing ball, and about a dozen families having picnics, and some people tossing a softball over there. They've all left."

Professor Childermass scowled. "Not so surprising. After all, it is getting on into the afternoon, and it's starting to look a little cloudy." His voice sounded uncertain. "Even holiday pleasures have to come to an end. Who wants to lug this basket back to the car?"

As Johnny turned to take the basket, he froze in sudden alarm. Off toward Emerson Street was a little grove of quaking aspens, and standing in the middle of it was the dark figure of Mergal. The man raised a thin stick, about five or six feet long. It was not perfectly straight, but looked as if it might be the sawed-off trunk of a sapling or perhaps a tree branch trimmed of all its twigs. He held this staff at one end, and for a moment it pointed straight up at the sky. Then Mergal swung the stick down in an arc and hit the ground. He immediately spun on his heel and strode away, disappearing behind the trees. Johnny squeaked out a frightened cry.

"Now what?" demanded the professor in a quarrelsome voice, looking up from the tablecloth he was folding. "Don't tell me you're seeing—good heavens, what a gust!"

A stiff east wind had sprung up, raising dust on the infield and snatching leaves from the trees. The paper plates and cups sailed off from the picnic table too quickly for any of them to do more than grab at them and miss. The professor's worn white linen tablecloth tore itself from his grasp and went dancing away, billowing as if an evil spirit had thrown it on as an early Halloween costume. Professor Childermass ran toward it, but the cloth puffed and twirled just beyond his reach. Johnny felt the hairs on his neck rising. The wind-dancing cloth was just like everyone's idea of a sheet-clad ghost, tricky and elusive and somehow threatening.

A wrack of grayish-purple clouds boiled up from the east and spread fantastically fast, obscuring the sun. "Gosh," Sarah said. "It's gonna storm, but the weatherman said—"

A bolt of lightning cut off her voice. It was dazzlingly bright, and it slammed to earth on the baseball field. Johnny gasped as a shock wave pounded the air from his lungs. An instant later a terribly loud thunderclap nearly shook them off their feet. Johnny and Sarah shrieked simultaneously. Fifty feet away the professor gave up his chase, and the tablecloth kited up over the treetops as it dashed into the troubled sky.

"Run, children!" Professor Childermass shouted. "Keep away from the trees and head for my car!" He came running back to snatch up the picnic hamper, and all of them dashed for cover as another blinding bolt struck not twenty yards away. Johnny clapped his hands over his ears and looked over his shoulder, only to see the concrete table where they had been eating split into fragments. Marble-sized pieces of concrete suddenly pelted to earth all around the fleeing trio, the fragments blackened and still smoking. They rushed up a grassy embankment to Emerson Street, and a hard rain began to lash them, a cold rain mixed with painful hail. The white pellets of ice thumped against their heads and backs and arms, stinging like small rocks.

The professor shielded his glasses with one hand. "This will never do. It's like being under fire from an army of Lilliputians!" They were still a block away from the maroon Pontiac. The rain slammed into them twice as hard as before, and hail the size of mothballs began to smack against the pavement. Professor Childermass seized the door handle of a beat-up blue Chevy sedan and wrenched the door open. "Pile in, both of you!"

Johnny and Sarah tumbled into the back seat, and Professor Childermass clambered into the front passenger seat. He slammed the door as the fierce hail clattered against the windshield and the top of the car. A vengeful wind rocked the car on its springs, as if the storm were trying to rip it apart to get at them. More sizzling bolts of lightning struck all around them, each so bright and so loud that the world suddenly turned white and the terrible, vibrating thunder exploded before the lightning had even faded.

Every time the lightning flashed, Johnny and Sarah screamed. "We're all right," Professor Childermass shouted. "We are in a vehicle insulated from the ground by four rubber tires. That makes us perfectly safe—"

Another bolt struck a maple ten yards away, blasting a cloud of wood splinters and leaves into the rain-streaked air. The professor did not scream. Instead, in a soft voice he rapidly recited the rulers of the Roman Empire and their reputed heirs from Julius Caesar to Kaiser Wilhelm and Czar Nicholas. Then he muttered a brief prayer to St. Michael. He did that only when something really bothered him.

Their panting breath fogged the car windows. The upholstery was split and ratty, and the air in the car smelled unpleasantly of engine oil and rust, but the banged-up old sedan was a welcome haven. Fortunately the furious storm lasted for only ten minutes before it blew away as suddenly as it had come. Billowing black clouds smoked away to the west, trailing skirts of rain. The sun peeked out again. All around, trees dangled broken limbs and dripped onto the soggy ground. "I think it's over," Johnny ventured.

"Possibly," returned Professor Childermass. "Let's get to my car, and I'll take you both home."

As they were leaving the Chevrolet, a frowning man ran up. He was about six feet tall and muscular, with a heavy, bristly jaw, a crooked nose, and two straight, jet-black eyebrows over his glaring brown eyes. "Hey," he said in a rough, menacing tone, "what's the idea? That's my car you was in!"

Professor Childermass drew himself up to his full five feet seven. Behind his gold-rimmed spectacles, his eyes glittered. He barked out his words: "My dear sir, stop apologizing! I refuse to listen to another word. Don't belittle your car—be proud of it!" Then, sounding kinder, he added, "Your somewhat worn sedan gave these defenseless children safety during the late meteorological disturbance. In fact, as automobiles go, it's even sort of a hero! So although your Chevrolet appears to be in a run-down, battered, and even disreputable condition, I must congratulate, not scold, you."

For a moment the man just looked puzzled. "Well—well, gosh, thanks!" he said at last with a shy grin.

The professor gave him a friendly handshake. "Think nothing of it. I know *I* won't. All right, troops!" he snapped. "Ahead, quick march!"

Johnny took a fearful look back. The park was a mess. Hail had beaten down the flower beds and had pummeled the baseball diamond to muddy mush. Lightning had splintered five or six trees, and the wind had ripped big branches off others. Leaves were scattered everywhere, on the grass, on the pavement, even plastered to all the cars parked nearby. The picnic table lay in shattered ruins. The rain-washed air had a scent of ozone, reminding Johnny of the way his electric-train set smelled when both engines were clattering around the track. "It was a magic storm," Johnny said quietly.

Sarah gave him a strange look. "Magic? Are you crazy?"

Johnny bit his lip. "I saw Mr. Mergal doing something with a—a wand, I guess it was. He summoned the storm somehow, I swear he did. And the lightning was *chasing* us."

"Not another word," Professor Childermass said in a warning tone. They climbed into his Pontiac, and as they rolled away from the devastated park, Johnny felt more frightened and worried than ever.

CHAPTER EIGHT

Sarah wanted to know all about Mr. Mergal, but for days Johnny put her off. He didn't want his new friend to start wondering if maybe he was a little nutty. The rest of the week passed, and then Monday came around again. It happened to be another delivery day, and Johnny settled down to what had become a normal routine.

This time, though, something was different about the Gudge Museum. It still had the creaks and groans of any old house, but Johnny kept thinking he heard something else, something soft and sly and sinister. It was exactly like hearing someone whisper from the next room, a maddening *s-ss-ss* of sound, with an occasional evil chuckle thrown in. But every time Johnny went to find the source of the noise, it seemed to be coming from the room he had just left. Sometimes Johnny was too imaginative for his own good. In his mind he conjured up all sorts of explanations for the unusual whispery sounds. It might be the mysterious Mr. Mergal, slipping from one hiding place to another, planning to murder him. It might be old Blackleach's ghost, roaming the halls of the museum, guarding his witchy treasures. It might even be the spirit of Sophonsoba Peabody, gliding sorrowfully from room to room, trying to find someone to listen to one of her terrible poems.

Whatever it was, Johnny grew more and more nervous listening to the sound. He tried to control his wild fantasies, telling himself that the noises were just the sound of tree leaves brushing against the wall outside, or the cranky old air-conditioning system getting ready to break down. Still, he was so jumpy that when the loading door buzzer sounded, he yelped and leaped off his chair. With a red face, he hurried to open the back door. It was just the delivery man, and he had Johnny sign for a box of soap and paper towels. Johnny hurriedly stored them away and then left for home.

He was jumpy all evening. He had dinner and then sat in the parlor and watched a Red Sox baseball game with his grandfather. The black-and-white television didn't have the greatest reception in the world, and the static was so bad that it was a little like watching a ball game played in the middle of a blinding blizzard. Unfortunately the Red Sox had not improved as the summer wore on. They lost to the Cleveland Indians, a team that was giving the New York Yankees a tough contest for the pennant that year.

It was a hot night, and after Johnny went to bed, he tossed and turned restlessly. His window was wide open, but the breezes that came in were sluggish and warm. His Big Ben alarm clock ticked and ticked, its monotonous metallic voice going on and on, like a boring speaker droning on about nothing. Every now and then a car would drive past, the reflection of its headlights making patterns of light and shadow move across his bedroom ceiling. Once a shadow vaguely like a hand crept above his bed, and Johnny turned onto his stomach and closed his eyes. Finally, after midnight Johnny drifted off to sleep. Some time later he began to dream.

In the dream he was working in the museum as usual, dusting the exhibits in the Peabody Room. He felt someone's eyes on him the whole time, and he got jittery. He kept thinking he heard someone whispering, and he looked this way and that, but he was all alone. Then, as he had finished carefully cleaning the vases on the mantel, he heard a low, nasty laugh behind him. "That's right, baby Johnny," said the taunting voice of Eddie Tompke. "Make 'em nice and pretty now!"

Johnny whirled, but no one was behind him. "Eddie? Darn it, where are you hiding? You're sure not s'posed to—"

"Here I am," said the voice from the other end of the mantel.

Johnny looked, and to his horror he saw a blue vase leap off the mantel and fly across the room. It shattered on the floor. The nasty voice said, "See, I learned how to become invisible, baby Johnny. I'm gonna make your life re-e-al interesting from now on!" And one, two, three other vases smashed against the wall. Then unseen hands began to rip the precious manuscripts of Sophonsoba Peabody's poetry. Fragments of sonnets and ballads whirled through the air like snow. And at that moment Miss Ferrington's harsh voice came from the corridor: "Johnny Dixon! Here I come!"

Johnny tried to run and found himself held back. Something was strangling him, choking him, as Eddie Tompke's laughter rang out. Desperately, Johnny lunged—

And fell out of bed, waking himself up. He was all tangled in his sheets, and he was sweating. He struggled up, angry at himself. What a baby! The luminous hands of his clock said that it was after 3:00 A.M. Johnny switched on his reading lamp to make his bed again. He was very fussy about certain things. They had to be just right. He hated sleeping in a rumpled bed, and he carefully made hospital corners as he tucked the sheet around the mattress.

He had put on his glasses to do this task. He switched off the light and then for some reason he looked out his window. He had a good view of Fillmore Street from up there. Everything looked spooky and deserted at this time of night. A high moon that he could not see cast a dim silvery light over the neighborhood. The professor's stucco mansion glimmered in the glow, looking unearthly, the way Johnny imagined Edgar Allan Poe's House of Usher looked even in the daylight. Except, he thought, the House of Usher probably did not have the square Italian cupola with the ridiculous radio aerial that his old friend's house sported.

The shadow of a small cloud drifted over the roof of the professor's house. Johnny yawned. Then he stiffened and leaned forward for a closer look, pressing his nose against the screen. *Was* that gliding black shape a shadow? It was hard to be sure. The patch of darkness came flowing down the roof and then moved onto the stucco wall.

Johnny's heart seemed to stop. The shadow had a definite shape. It looked like a man, dressed all in black from head to foot. And it clung to the stucco wall just like an insect. It scuttled around, hanging head down, then moving sideways, exactly as a fly might creep over the frosted surface of a cake. It seemed to be fiddling with a window screen.

Johnny leaped up and ran downstairs. He switched on a light and grabbed the telephone. His hand was shaking, but he managed to dial the professor's number. It rang once, then twice. "Come on, Professor," groaned Johnny. Three times. Four.

After the seventh ring, the professor picked up the phone. "Hello!" he roared in his crabbiest voice. "Whoever this is, I hope you're calling about an emergency.

Someone had better be on the way to the hospital, at least!"

"Professor!" said Johnny. "It's me! There's a guy tryin' to climb in your bedroom window!"

"Johnny?" muttered the professor in a surprised voice. "The devil you say! Hold on—if I'm not back in five minutes, call the police!"

Johnny was not wearing his watch. He tried counting seconds the way he had learned in the Boy Scouts, murmuring, "One, one thousand, two, one thousand, three, one thousand, four . . . "

He lost count at two minutes and something and was about to hang up and call the police anyway when the professor picked up the phone again. "False alarm, John," he said in a tired voice. "No one's there. What made you think someone was trying to break in?"

Johnny stammered out his strange story, realizing that it sounded as if the shadow had been part of his bad dream. "It was there. I mean, it was real, not just my imagination. And, Professor, he went down the wall like he had suction cups for hands and feet!"

"You don't say," responded Professor Childermass. "Isn't that odd?"

"What?"

"At the very instant you called and woke me, I was just starting one of my lovely dreams about that creepy-crawly hand. Ugh! I wonder—good heavens, look at the time! You go right back to bed, John, and don't worry about any weird interlopers. I can take care of myself. But thank you for phoning me. You probably saved me from a doozy of a nightmare."

The phone clicked, and Johnny hung up the receiver. He went back to his bedroom with dread in his heart. What if the menacing black shadow had been some sort of spirit or spell instead of a person? And what if it somehow *knew* he had called the professor? Would it visit his home next, climb down the wall outside his room, softly pry off the screen over his window?

Shivering despite the heat, Johnny huddled in his bed. After a long time he fell asleep again and this time did not dream.

Naturally Johnny felt groggy and cranky the next morning. Gramma had made some delicious oatmeal-raisin bread, and she toasted him a couple of big slices to go with his scrambled egg and bacon. Johnny didn't have much appetite, though, and soon he left to go to the museum.

He rode his bike downtown and along Merrimack Street toward the river. On a Tuesday morning in mid-July, everything was sleepy and slow, but that all changed as Johnny came within sight of the museum. A police car was parked outside the front door. With a creepy feeling of déjà vu, Johnny pedaled faster. He parked his bike and hurried around to the front and up the steps.

He heard Miss Ferrington's wail as he pushed the door open: "It's terrible! Nothing like this has ever happened! And it isn't my fault!"

"Well, gosh, Miss Ferrington, nobody said it was!" It was a young man's voice, but Johnny did not recognize the speaker.

"But just think of what might have happened! The Sophonsoba Peabody pieces are irreplaceable! If they had only known how valuable they were, the museum might have been ruined, desecrated, vandalized!"

What in the world was going on? Johnny paused outside the office door and gave a hesitant knock. For a moment everyone inside was quiet. Then the door opened. Miss Ferrington glared at him for a second or two. Then she turned and said, "Here he is! Johnny Dixon is responsible! And the little hoodlum comes walking in as if he owns the place!"

Johnny backed away, his heart pounding and his throat dry.

A policeman came to stand behind Miss Ferrington. He was young and looked irritable. He carried a clipboard in one hand. "Now, wait," he said. "We don't have any evidence that—"

"He left the door unlocked!" shouted Miss Ferrington. "He's probably the ringleader of a whole band of hooligans! Officer, arrest this boy! Johnny Dixon is the thief!"

For a moment Johnny just stood there with his mouth hanging open, staring at the furious Miss Ferrington and unable even to speak. Then terror raced through him. Without even meaning to do it, he spun and ran. He flew down the steps, raced around the corner, and unlocked his bike. By the time the young policeman was standing in the open doorway of the museum and yelling, "Hey, you!" Johnny was already speeding away. His legs pumped the pedals furiously. He did not know where he was going or what he was planning to do. He only knew that he was in serious trouble, that he was now a fugitive, and that the police were coming after him.

CHAPTER NINE

A terrified Johnny pedaled to the professor's house, turned in at the potholed driveway, and jumped off his bike. He leaped up the porch steps two at a time and pounded on the door. "Professor! Professor! You gotta help me!" yelled Johnny, his voice cracking.

The professor opened the door, a look of astonishment on his red face. He was in baggy gray cotton trousers, an open-collared blue shirt, and his scruffy old navy-blue terrycloth slippers. "What on earth is wrong, John?" he asked, his eyes round with wonder.

"M-Miss F-Ferrington th-thinks I stole something!" stammered Johnny, tears in his eyes. "Sh-she has the p-police after me, but I didn't, Professor. I swear to God I didn't!"

"Calm down," said the professor in a kindly voice. "I can hardly understand what you're saying. Miss Ferrington thinks you stole something?" When Johnny nodded miserably, the professor looked angry. "Why, that's preposterous! What are you supposed to have pilfered from that museum, better described as Junkpile Manor?"

"I don't know," confessed Johnny. "D-do you th-think they'll send me to jail?" He imagined jail as a dark brick closet, with rats and spiders creeping around in the smelly dankness.

"Certainly not!" exploded the professor. "Give me a minute to get into some more suitable clothes, and then let's march right over to your house, John Michael. When trouble comes, I always believe you should face right up to it. And don't worry. You have plenty of good friends, and we know you'd never steal so much as a paper clip from the Gudge Museum."

The professor made Johnny come inside and sit in the new armchair in the living room while he went upstairs for his shoes, tie, and jacket. Johnny began to weep. Not because he was so frightened, but because he had seen tears glistening in the professor's eyes too. He knew that what Professor Childermass said was true. Gramma and Grampa would just about give up their lives for Johnny, and so would the professor and Fergie. The thought of having friends like that overwhelmed Johnny, and he cried partly out of a reaction to his fear and uncertainty, but mostly out of relief.

A more presentably dressed professor came downstairs, nodded grimly, and said, "Let's go." The two of them hurried across Fillmore Street, where the professor summoned Johnny's grandmother and grandfather to what he called a council of war. They sat at the oak table in the kitchen and a hesitant Johnny did his best to explain what had happened. The professor could not sit still, but paced, humming unmusically, as he often did when angry or worried. When Johnny's explanation trailed off, everyone was quiet. The red electric clock made a buzzing sound that seemed loud in the silence.

"I can get to the bottom of this," announced the professor, and he went to make a telephone call. After a few minutes he returned, rubbing his hands. "Everyone can relax. The police are *not* after Johnny, despite what he heard Miss Ferrington say. They don't believe Johnny was in on the heist."

Grampa raised his eyebrows and scratched his bald head. He frowned and asked, "In on th' *what*, Rod?"

The professor looked impatient. "The heist. You know, the caper." He read a lot of mystery stories, and he thought that policemen and criminals talked like that. When he saw that Grampa still didn't have a glimmer of what he meant, the professor puffed out his cheeks, rolled his eyes, and in an exasperated voice said, "The burglary, to put it in plain English."

Gramma, a short, white-haired woman, put her hand against her chest. "Mercy sakes! Somebody robbed the Gudge Museum? What did they steal, Professor?"

"According to the police," the professor said, "the

criminal had a strangely discriminating taste. The burglar lifted only items from the Colonial Curiosities Room, and at that, he took only the ones that I had lent to the museum. So the yegg, or as you would probably call him, the thief, got away with a boxful of crummy junk that he could probably fence for, oh, maybe eleven dollars and seventeen cents."

A shock ran through Johnny. "Professor!" he exclaimed. "That means—"

The professor gave him a warning look. "That means that the burglar was dumb enough to think that those stupid old geegaws were actually worth good American money," he said firmly. "But *we* know he was mistaken."

Johnny realized that the professor did not want him to mention Mr. Mergal in front of Gramma and Grampa. He swallowed his words and nodded.

"Well, Rod," asked Grampa, "why did th' woman think Johnny took her old rubbish, anyway?"

Professor Childermass made a face. "From what the police say, it's because he worked late yesterday and was the last one to leave. Johnny was supposed to lock up the museum before he went home."

"I did!" said Johnny. "I remember trying to pull the front door open, an' it was locked tight!"

"How about the back door?" asked the professor.

Johnny frowned. "The loading-dock door? Well, that one has to be opened with a key all the time. I mean, if you open it with a key and then close it, it locks automatically."

"Are you sure you pushed the door all th' way shut?" asked Gramma, looking worried. "Mightn't you have made a mistake, Johnny?"

Johnny shook his head. "I know it was locked when I left. That door has a whatchamacallit, a closer on it, that pulls it shut. I heard it click, I know I did."

"I believe Johnny," said Grampa, laying a big hand on his grandson's shoulder.

"Of course you do," returned the professor. "So do I. My heavens, if they need a character witness, Father Higgins will be glad to testify to Johnny's honesty. You can't get a much better reference than a priest!"

"Still, even honest people can make mistakes," said Gramma.

"Be that as it may," returned the professor calmly, "Miss Ferrington swears that the back door was ajar this morning. It was propped open, and also someone had jammed the lock, so it couldn't close properly."

"I didn't do it!" Johnny insisted.

The professor patted him on the shoulder. "Of course you didn't. Now, don't worry. You see, I own all the things that are missing from the museum. Even if you left the front door open with a sign on it saying, 'Hey, crooks, come in and help yourselves,' I would have to file a complaint for the police to bother you. And I have no intention of complaining about losing that miserable heap of trash. My frivolous brother Perry had no right to saddle me with all that ghastly garbage, anyway. Good riddance is what I say."

But Gramma and Grampa were still troubled, so the professor said he would take Johnny down to the police station and "put the fix in." They walked downtown, and on the way Professor Childermass warned Johnny, "I'm sorry I stepped in so abruptly back there, but our charming Mr. Mergal is no one your grandparents should be worrying about. Let me deal with him, and everything will be all right."

"Do you think he did it, Professor?" asked Johnny in a small voice. He hated this walk to the police station, and he still had a lingering fear that they might throw him in a cell and give him the third degree.

"Do I think Mr. Mergal stole the Blackleach exhibits?" mused the professor. "Well, let me put it this way: a big, fat yes! And do I think our police force will pin the crime on him? Not in a million, billion, gazillion years. No doubt our clever, felonious friend has set up some cozy little alibi, just as he did after ransacking my house. Probably he will claim to have been in Bombay admiring a white elephant, or in Katmandu chatting with a lama, or maybe in Marie Byrd Land hobnobbing with some emperor penguins."

"What does he want with all that stuff?" asked Johnny.

The professor sighed. "Lord knows. Dr. Coote has worked hard gathering together all the old manuscript books on the evil wizard Blackleach, but I haven't read through them yet. I will owe Charley a delicious dinner at some first-class restaurant when this is all over. He's taking time out from correcting the proofs of his voo-doo book to research these things for me."

They went into the police station, and in a small room a young plainclothes police officer came in to talk to them. He had sandy brown hair, a long nose, and eye-brows that were so high they made him look a little astonished all the time. He introduced himself as Ser-geant Mike Kluczykowski and listened politely to John-ny's story. Then Sergeant Kluczykowski pulled his nose thoughtfully, as if it were not yet quite long enough to suit him. "Hmm. I see. Well, Miss Ferrington reported that she came in this morning to unlock and she felt a breeze. She went down the hallway and into that little alcove, and there she found the back door open. It was propped with a brick. She tried to close it—that was a silly thing to do, because we want civilians to leave a crime scene alone—and the lock wouldn't click. Some-one had jammed a small piece of gravel in the latch plate. She went through the whole museum and discovered that the exhibits in the Curiosities Room were missing, and then she called us in." He gave Johnny a rueful smile. "I don't really think you are to blame, but I'm afraid Miss Ferrington is pretty mad. You've probably lost your job." The sergeant turned to the professor. "Now, since you own those antiques, I guess it's up to you to give us a description of them."

"There's really no need of that. I don't want to press charges," the professor told him.

The young policeman tugged at his nose once again.

"Well, that's a little awkward, because you see, breaking and entering is a crime. In fact, it is a felony, which means we can't drop our investigation, whether you want your stuff back or not. So I'll have to insist that you give us a description of the missing items."

Professor Childermass grumbled a bit, but he finally agreed. A black-haired young woman carrying a stenographer's pad came in and took down the information. At last Sergeant Kluczykowski thanked them for their help and told them they could go. The two friends walked back to Fillmore Street together. The professor was in a bad mood and he was smoking one of his Balkan Sobranies as they strode along. Johnny didn't have the courage to remind him that he was trying to quit. Now that Johnny knew the police didn't intend to put him in solitary confinement, he felt better. Still, he sensed that he was in for more trouble.

When they turned onto Fillmore Street, Johnny saw Sarah Channing sitting on his front porch steps. "Oh, no," he groaned. "Now I'll have to tell her the whole story. Professor, what do you think I ought to do about my job?"

Professor Childermass shook his head hopelessly. "Well, John, I'm afraid the policeman was right. Miss Ferrington isn't one to forgive and forget, so she probably will fire you. I'll call her if you wish. Unfortunately, with brother Perry's marvelous magical mementos now missing, I have nothing to bargain with. However, when we pin this job on dear Mr. Mergal, I'll do everything I can to get you back into whatever good graces the lady has."

"Hey, Dixon!" shouted Sarah as they approached. "I heard about the burglary on the radio, so I went right over to the museum." She came jogging up. In a quieter voice she said, "Only Miss Ferrington told me you don't work there anymore. Is that true?"

"Yeah," said Johnny miserably. "Yeah, I guess it's true." It had been a long time since he had felt this heartbroken. He had let everyone down: Miss Ferrington, of course, but even worse, Professor Childermass, Gramma, and Grampa too. He could only hope that the professor was right and that somehow he could clear his good name and find the real thief.

But at the moment that seemed like a forlorn hope.

CHAPTER TEN

The big showdown came two days later, when Sarah finally persuaded Johnny to confide his worries to her. Johnny had received his last pay envelope in the mail. It wasn't very much money, but it reminded him of the job he had lost, and thinking about Miss Ferrington's accusations depressed him. When Sarah telephoned to chat, Johnny admitted he was unhappy.

Sarah listened with sympathy and then suggested that he teach her how to play chess, something they had talked about before. Maybe it would take Johnny's mind off his troubles for a little while. He didn't really think it would, but then it might be sort of cheerful to play again. He and Fergie always played hard-fought, interesting games of chess, and the professor was usually a good opponent. But with Fergie away and the professor preoccupied, Johnny hadn't touched his chessboard in weeks.

He met Sarah at the public library, and they set up Johnny's chessboard in the Conversation Room on the first floor. Quiet talking was allowed there, and lots of people met there to play chess or checkers. Sometimes spectators even collected in small audiences to watch games and debate each move in whispers. Johnny was glad to see no one was there, because he felt self-conscious about playing chess in front of people. He arranged the pieces on the board. Sarah watched as Johnny explained how each chess piece could move, and then she moved them herself, making sure she understood.

Next Johnny explained what a gambit was—a series of beginning chess moves that could be developed into an attack or a defense. There were lots of standard openings, but they would begin with very simple ones. Then he hid a couple of pawns in his hands, and she chose the hand that held the white one. "Okay," he said. "White always moves first. Now, the first time you move a pawn, it can go either one or two squares. I'd start with the one in front of the queen or the king."

And then as they moved the chessmen, Sarah started in again, asking about Mattheus Mergal and what he had to do with the storm in the park. "I didn't see him, but he really gave you the creeps, didn't he?" she asked.

Trying not to show either annoyance or anxiety,

Johnny kept his gaze on the board. "Yeah, I guess he did. He's a peculiar guy."

Sarah stared over the chess pieces, frowning at him. "Weird how? Does he run through the streets in his underwear, playing a banjo and singing 'Hail, Columbia'? Does he turn into a werewolf when the wolfsbane blooms, and the moon is shining bright?"

"Let's just play chess, okay?" Johnny did not feel like talking about Mattheus Mergal. For one thing, he was a mystery, and Johnny did not know all that much. Then too, Johnny had a bad feeling that no matter what he said, Sarah would misunderstand.

But Sarah would not let the matter drop. As they moved their chess pieces, she kept asking questions, and she refused to let Johnny get away with shrugging them off. Little by little she wore down Johnny's reluctance.

Finally Johnny sighed and dropped his voice to a whisper, "Okay, okay, but you'll never believe me." He took a deep breath. "It all goes back to the witch things." He told her about Esdrias Blackleach. Then he said, "I think Mr. Mergal wants to get all of Blackleach's magical stuff so he can cast spells too. He must have been the one who broke into the professor's house and later stole all the Blackleach pieces from the museum. He got me fired, and I think he tried to kill the professor with that magic lightning in the park."

Sarah frowned at him for a few moments. Then she

grinned, her eyes crinkling. She chuckled, in the way that people do when they think something funny is about to happen. "What's the joke, Dixon?" she asked.

Johnny scowled at her. "I knew you wouldn't believe me," he muttered.

"Well, who in the world would?" demanded Sarah, irritation flashing in her eyes. "You *are* kidding, aren't you? I mean, about magic."

How could he tell her about the things he had seen, about zombies and ghosts and trolleys that could go back in time? Sarah had never encountered the sort of bizarre people who seemed to be attracted to Duston Heights like iron to a magnet. "Just forget it," said Johnny wearily.

Sarah moved her knight. It was a bad move, opening up her queen to a bishop attack. She glanced back at him and seemed surprised at his bitter expression. "Oh, come on, Dixon. Nobody believes in wizards and witches and that kinda stuff." She sounded like a big sister talking to a six-year-old brat of a little brother. "Is this Mergal guy just plain nuts?"

Johnny ignored the chance to take Sarah's queen. "I guess he is. He thinks Blackleach was a real magician, and he wants to be a magician too. We know there's no such thing as magic, so let's just forget about him, okay?"

Sarah gave him a quizzical glance. "This really bothers you. Okay, Dixon, convince me. Why do you think

Blackleach's snow globe and the other little toys have spooky power? What makes you think Mergal has malicious magic on his mind?"

"I *told* you I saw him at the park," insisted Johnny. His voice had risen and it almost squeaked. He made an effort to speak more softly. "He was holdin' some kind of long staff, and he raised it up to point at the sky, and then he struck the ground with it. And right after that, those weird clouds came boiling up out of nowhere and the lightning began."

"But thunderstorms happen in the summer," Sarah objected. "That one could've just been a coincidence."

"Witches are supposed to be able to raise storms," insisted Johnny.

"Oh, Dixon, I don't believe in witches. And I didn't see Mergal do any funny business with a staff. Maybe you just imagined you saw him—"

Johnny glared at her. "I'm sorry I told you anything. Just forget it."

"But—"

With a quick, spiteful movement Johnny swept his bishop diagonally across the board and took Sarah's queen. "There! You didn't watch what you were doing, and I captured your most important piece. Are you going to concentrate now?"

"That was mean!"

Johnny gave her a crabby look. "I think you're pretty mean to say I'm crazy 'cause I think that Mergal is trying to do witchcraft. Maybe it doesn't really work, maybe *he*'s off his rocker, but that doesn't mean I am."

Sarah looked angry. "If you're gonna be that way, Johnny Dixon, I don't want to play this stupid game anymore."

Johnny felt like yelling, but he kept his voice quiet. "It's not a stupid game just because you're too dumb to learn how to play it!"

Sarah glowered at him. Then she got up and stalked out of the Conversation Room. Angry at himself, Johnny folded the board and packed it and the chess pieces back in the box. He trudged back to Fillmore Street with the dejected sense that he had just lost a friend. He spent the rest of the day in his room, trying to read and listening to his old Motorola radio. That night he thought long and hard about everything that had happened. If only there was some way of catching Mr. Mergal in the act, or finding some of the loot from the museum in his possession!

But he had no idea of how to do that. If Fergie were here, he thought, he'd know what to do. Even if he didn't believe Mergal was an evil magician, Fergie would come up with some plan to discover exactly what mischief he was trying to pull. Unfortunately, Fergie was still hundreds of miles away, and Johnny didn't have his friend's willingness to take chances. He wished he were braver and older. He wished he could live up to Professor Childermass' idea of him—the professor always treated Johnny like a sensible adult, not a child. But surrounded by a troublesome cloud of doubts and regrets, Johnny felt very childlike indeed.

Professor Childermass sympathized with Johnny, but he couldn't offer much help. "After all," he said, "you wouldn't want to involve Sarah in anything dangerous, would you? And if jolly old Mr. Mergal really is trying to gain control of evil magical powers, he could be pretty dangerous." The two of them sat in the professor's kitchen, waiting for a pan of dark-chocolate walnut fudge to harden. It was the day after Sarah and Johnny had quarrelled in the public library. Although he hadn't said a word about the fight to Gramma or Grampa, Johnny had told the professor everything. The old man was his good friend, and sometimes it's easier to talk about certain things to friends.

Johnny was sipping a tall, cool glass of milk, and the professor was drinking a steaming cup of coffee. His eyes glittered shrewdly behind his gold-rimmed glasses as he said, "You know, John, maybe it's better that you and Sarah stay away from each other for a few days. I expect that if you give it time, she'll decide that you both were a little too hasty."

"I didn't want to hurt her feelings," admitted Johnny. "But I don't think she'll be my friend again. She thinks I'm cranky and maybe crazy too."

"She does, does she?" asked Professor Childermass, looking concerned. "You might have a problem there. Of course, I don't mind the good citizens of Duston

Heights thinking I'm cranky. In fact, I rather enjoy it, because it keeps a lot of irritating, obnoxious people away. But at your age you shouldn't have that kind of reputation. John, I'll tell you what: When this is over, I'll invite Sarah and you to another picnic and we'll smooth things over. After all, they say time heals all wounds."

"I hope it does," replied Johnny. "Sarah was kind of a special friend."

"Your first girlfriend?" asked the professor.

"No!" Johnny frowned. "I mean, she's a girl and she's my friend, but that's all."

"I hope all this will be over in a week or two," said the professor. He got up and took the fudge from the pan. "Here, sample this."

The candy was creamy and delicious, and Johnny nodded to show that it was a success. He swallowed and said, "What do you mean, you hope it's gonna be over in a week or two? What are you planning, Professor?"

But Professor Childermass just winked. "Don't fret about it. There are wheels within wheels, as the saying goes, and if all the wheels roll along as they should, I'll prove to the authorities that Mr. Mattheus Mergal of Boston, Massachusetts, is the villain who's committed two burglaries. And if that doesn't settle the fellow's hash, I don't know what will!"

Johnny was still far from satisfied, but he made up his mind to wait and see. He simply didn't know what other choice he had.

CHAPTER ELEVEN

Days went by. Johnny moped around the house, did chores for his grandparents, spent hours in his room, and daydreamed that he was Sergeant John M. Dixon of Gangbusters, and that he and a carload of tough cops would come roaring up with sirens blasting to arrest Mr. Mattheus Mergal. They would catch him in the act of robbing a bank. He would snarl, "You'll never take me alive, coppers!"

Then, in a hail of tommy-gun fire, Johnny would dash into the building, yelling, "Cover me, boys!" After crashing through the door, he would get into a wild fist-fight with Mergal, thrashing him until the coward broke down and confessed that he was to blame for everything. The bank would be full of hostages, and Miss Ferrington would be one of them. She would weep and beg Johnny to forgive her. He wasn't quite sure if he would or not.

But when the daydream was over, Johnny had to admit that it was a fantasy. He began to be afraid that maybe Sarah was right. Maybe he had lost his marbles. He wished he could come up with some way to prove that his worries were about real things and not just in his mind.

One morning Johnny came downstairs and heard voices in the parlor. He recognized the professor's querulous voice and Grampa Dixon's mild tones. Johnny knew eavesdropping was wrong, but something made him stop and listen.

"Rod, if it was just that he was feelin' a little down, I could understand," Grampa Dixon was saying. "I guess everybody feels that way now an' again. But he's been draggin' around for days. Kate wants me to take him to Doc Schermerhorn for a checkup, because she's afraid he might be comin' down with infantile paralysis or somethin'. What do you think?"

The professor replied, "Henry, John is just growing up, that's all. When you were his age, didn't you have bleak days when the whole world seemed against you? Didn't you ever get into silly quarrels with your friends?"

"I s'pose I did," replied Johnny's grandfather slowly. "Only Johnny's always been such a loner. Y' know, I think he really misses Fergie. For a while we thought that maybe he an' that nice Sarah Channing girl were gonna become good friends, but he hasn't talked about her much lately."

"Give him a little time," the professor said.

"Then y' don't think we should take him to Doc Schermerhorn?"

Johnny heard Professor Childermass snort. "Henry, I wouldn't take a sick cat to that quack. I haven't trusted him since he told my cousin Bea she was having headaches because her teeth were bad, and then a couple of months later she died of a brain tumor. Besides, his jokes are so terrible they give patients nervous stomachs, hives, and the blind staggers. I'm busy now, but in a week or two, certainly by August, I'll take Johnny down to Boston for a few Red Sox games. That will take his mind off his miseries, and before long Fergie will be back, and everything will return to normal."

"Y' think so, Rod?"

"I'm positive, Henry."

Johnny coughed, and the two men fell silent as he walked into the parlor. Grampa Dixon looked a little embarrassed, the way he sometimes looked if he and the professor were sitting at the kitchen table sipping whiskey and Gramma walked in. Gramma did not approve of alcohol. "Hi, Johnny," mumbled Grampa Dixon. "Say, Rod here was just wonderin' if you'd wanta go to see the Red Sox play sometime."

"That'd be swell," said Johnny, but he could not put much enthusiasm into his reply.

"How are you feeling, John?" asked Professor Childermass.

Johnny shrugged. "Okay, I guess. I thought I'd cut the grass today, before it gets hot."

"Good idea," said the professor. "In fact, if you want, you can mow my lawn. I'll pay you two dollars. And if you uncover any chests of Spanish gold, you may keep them." The professor grinned.

Johnny smiled too, but his heart wasn't in it. He kept busy that day and the next morning with the yard work. The professor was being very mysterious, hopping in his car, driving away, and coming back at odd hours. He would not discuss what he was up to, and this made Johnny feel more left out than ever.

One afternoon Johnny walked downtown toward Peter's Sweet Shop. He saw Eddie Tompke and a bunch of his friends go into the shop, though, and he turned around to go back home. He didn't want to mix it up with them, not after the disturbing nightmares he had been having about Eddie.

But Sarah had just come around the corner, and she stopped, staring at him. "Hi," she said, and then she bit her lip.

"Hi," muttered Johnny. He walked past her, but she fell in beside him.

"Look, I've got something to tell you," she said. "I don't know if it's important or not, but I think you ought to know."

Johnny didn't reply or look at her. He felt a dull burning inside. Why couldn't she just leave him alone? "What?" he asked in a cranky voice.

"Your Mr. Mergal has moved to Duston Heights," she said.

Stopping dead in his tracks, Johnny stared at her. "Are you sure?"

Sarah nodded. "I know Mikey Bonner. He delivers the *Gazette*, and he said Mr. Mergal moved into an old empty house on Saltonstall Street last Friday or Saturday. On Monday Mike tried to get him to subscribe to the newspaper, and Mergal chased him away. Mikey was still complaining about it when we played flies an' grounders."

Johnny frowned. Saltonstall Street was closer to the Merrimack River than Fillmore Street, but it was in the same section of town. He tried to remember any empty houses. "Is that the one close to the old church?"

"Which church?"

Johnny rolled his eyes. "The old Congregational Church. It caught fire and the roof burned back in 1943, Grampa says. They never fixed it 'cause they built the new church on the other side of town."

"I don't know anything about the church," Sarah reminded him. "I'm new in town, remember?"

"Yeah." Johnny thought hard. "There's the old Bradstreet house. All the kids call it the haunted house, because it's big and creepy, all weathered gray, and it has this strange tower in the front—"

"That's it," said Sarah. "Mike said Mergal moved into a haunted house."

Johnny shivered. He and Fergie had often strolled past the old Victorian house. It was about a quarter mile past the ruined church, behind a forbidding fence of black wrought-iron. The overgrown yard sprouted chest-high weeds, and the bleak, dirty windows gazed out blearily, like evil eyes. A wooden sign hung drunkenly from the wrought-iron gate:

No Trespassing
Violators Will Be Prosecuted

Fergie had often dared Johnny to spend a night in the place. Kids around town told all sorts of stories about it. In the 1890's a crazy killer had hacked a man to pieces there, and they said that every night at midnight a puddle of blood formed in the front hall where the victim had fallen. People said that a spiral staircase led up into the tower, and if you walked up when the full moon was shining, you would see a shadowy form leap from the top and plummet down, only to be jerked short by a rope around its neck. That was the ghost of a woman who had committed suicide by hanging herself in the tower. Sometimes through the windows you could glimpse a ghostly coffin, drifting eerily from room to room. It would chase you, people said, and if it caught you, it snapped you up and sank into the earth, burying you alive.

Johnny had never been tempted to take Fergie's dare. He swallowed hard and said, "I know the house."

"Wanna go there?"

"No!" Johnny yelped the word out so loudly that it made Sarah jump.

"Take it easy, Dixon! If you're still mad at me—"

"I'm not," said Johnny miserably. "It's just that—well, I've seen Mr. Mergal. He's *weird*, Sarah. Something about him isn't right. I don't think we should go rushing over to his house. Maybe we could talk to the professor, and he might have some idea of what we should do."

"Hey, it's a free country," returned Sarah. "I mean, Mr. Mergal can move to Duston Heights if he wants to, right? And we can walk down Saltonstall Street if *we* want to. I'm not saying we should try to run Mr. Mergal down with our bikes or bop him on the bean with sling-shots or anything. All I wanted to do was take a look at that house. It's supposed to be pretty weird itself, from what I hear. And maybe we could get a glimpse of Mr. Mergal. After all, we just have Mikey's word for it. We don't really know that it's the same guy who spooked you in the museum."

"It would just about have to be," muttered Johnny. Mergal was an odd name. Two Mergals showing up in a small town like Duston Heights was too big a coincidence to swallow.

Sarah sniffed. "Dixon, I'll make you a deal. Go along with me and take a look at the house, and we can be friends again. But don't try to tell me this Mergal guy is gonna start howling at the moon or anything, okay?"

Taking a deep breath, Johnny nodded. He hadn't wanted to talk about magic and witchcraft anyway, but it would do no good to remind Sarah of that. The two of them walked across town, then turned onto Saltonstall Street.

The houses here were big and run-down. Many had been built back in the 1880's, when lots of people in Duston Heights were getting rich in the leather and shoe businesses. These were Victorian houses, with complex gables, porches, and gingerbread decorations, but most needed paint and repairs. A porch rail was broken here, a loose shutter hung crookedly there, and the yards were seedy and overgrown.

Bradstreet Hill was at the end of the street. The hill was a good place for sledding in a winter snowfall. At its crown was the silhouette of the old burned-out church. Johnny and Sarah plodded up the hill and paused to look at the ruin.

All the brick walls of the church still stood. The roof over the sanctuary had burned and collapsed onto the pews, and through the gaping hole where the front doors had been they could see charred timbers and piles of ashes with weeds sprouting from them. The church had been T-shaped, and the sanctuary was the vertical stroke of the T. The crossbar, containing the choir and the Sunday-school rooms, still looked intact. Of course, everything was far gone with decay and neglect, because the building had stood open to all kinds of weather for about ten years.

A long way past the church on the right was the last house on Saltonstall Street before it turned into a county highway and wound past cornfields and scattered farms. It was the Bradstreet house, and it huddled behind its black wrought-iron fence, looking forbidding and evil.

All around the brooding house grew a heavy thatch of unmowed grass. A thick layer of grime blinded all the windows. The place looked as if no one had lived there for fifty years.

Weathered to a dull gray, the house had been built in two big blocks. Facing the street was a long porch supported by thin Corinthian columns, with scalloped decorations running between them. The porch rail had rotted away, and now only a few broken banisters jutted this way and that, like decayed, snaggly teeth. Above the porch were two more stories, with narrow, tall windows framed by moldering shutters. At the steep roof peak, ornate lightning rods, iron spears with purple and red glass globes along their lengths, thrust up to the sky.

A second porch was over on the right side, where another three-storied section of the house projected into the yard. Between the two big blocks nestled a tower. Up to the roof line it was square, but then its top story became an octagonal cupola. An unusual lightning rod was on the steepled crown of the tower, with three red glass balls at the base and a large blue one at the top, supporting the spire. It looked like this:

"Are you sure he's there?" asked Johnny.

"Mikey said he was." But Sarah sounded uncertain, as if she couldn't believe anyone would live in a terrible place like that.

A crow swooped over their heads and sailed up to perch on a windowsill. It was a narrow ledge, and the big bird had to flap and scrabble with its claws to hold on. It pecked at the window hard, three times—tap! tap! tap!—then screeched a raucous caw! and flew away.

"Let's go knock on the door," said Sarah.

"Are you nuts?" returned Johnny.

"What harm can it do? Look, if he gets mad and blows his top, we can always say we're selling candy or something. Come on!" She pushed at the gate, and the metal hinges groaned as it swung inward.

"Sarah," pleaded Johnny. Too late. She was already halfway to the porch. Johnny hurried after her, staring anxiously at the weathered old house. It waited with a patient, sinister air, like a tiger watching its prey approach. The wooden porch steps creaked as Sarah stepped on them. "I don't like this," Johnny muttered, joining her on the porch. The rotten old boards underfoot sagged as if they were about to break, and a choking, nasty-smelling dust rose from them.

"Okay, we're selling candy for St. Michael's," muttered Sarah. "We'll knock and see if he's home and ask to take his order. Ready?"

Whether Johnny was ready or not, Sarah pounded on the door. Her fist made a dismal, echoing boom! boom! boom! The sound almost made Johnny jump out of his skin.

Then he felt the hairs on his neck bristle. The door opened. Slowly, with a protest of ancient, rusty hinges, it swung inward, into darkness. But no one was there.

"Want to explore?" asked Sarah. She put her foot on the threshold.

Johnny grabbed her arm. "No! There is something wrong about this—"

Sarah screamed. Johnny's jaw fell open as he stared into the darkness. From the deep gloom someone was coming toward them—someone or something. It was as tall as a man, but it moved with a shambling, loose step, as if it were about to fall apart.

And then it stumbled close enough for the light from the open door to fall on it.

It was a walking skeleton, dressed in the flaking scraps of a Pilgrim suit, with a tall, conical hat atop its pale, grinning skull. Ancient, dried shreds of moldy green flesh stuck to its cheeks, and cobwebs busy with spiders filled its eye sockets. The long, tattered coat that it wore hung open, and inside the skeleton's rib cage gray shapes moved, huge, red-eyed rats that gnawed the bones with their yellow teeth. The skeleton thrust its arms out as if it were blind in the light, and Johnny saw that its left hand was missing. The shape lurched forward, its jaws gaping, a hollow groan coming from its bony mouth—

Johnny pulled Sarah away, and they leaped off the porch. Behind them they heard an angry snarl, and as they ran through the tall grass, *things* writhed at their feet.

Snakes! Hundreds of snakes reared, hissed, coiled, and struck at them. Sarah shrieked at the top of her lungs, and Johnny thought he was going to faint. He stepped on a muscular body that bulged and twisted underfoot, and with a yelp he rushed forward. He and Sarah reached the iron gate, but a huge, scaly green serpent coiled itself in and out of the bars, its evil triangular head raised, its slitted blood-red eyes glaring at them. It struck as Johnny pushed Sarah through the open gate, its fangs barely missing them. An instant later they were outside.

When Johnny looked behind him, all the snakes had

vanished. "They weren't real!" he gasped. "It was some kinda trick—look!"

Sarah was breathing hard and shaking so badly, she could hardly stand. The two of them were shoulder to shoulder, staring back through the iron gate at the gray old house, its door peacefully closed. "That—that *thing* in the house. Do you think that was real?"

"I don't know," Johnny confessed. "But I'm never going back in there as long as I live!"

From behind them a grating voice said, "Oh, you didn't enjoy your visit, hmm? Come back any time—I never lock my gate!"

Johnny and Sarah wheeled around. Not three steps away stood the tall, gaunt, black-suited figure of Mattheus Mergal. His stained, uneven teeth showed in a fierce grin. From overhead, the crow screamed again, an evil, nails-on-a-blackboard sound.

"Well, if you really must go, there is the way," Mergal said, stepping aside and gesturing down the hill.

Sarah and Johnny began to run at the same instant. They ran as if the devil himself were at their heels.

CHAPTER TWELVE

They stopped at the intersection of Saltonstall and Main streets, gasping for breath. "H-h-he's not f-following us, is he?" panted Johnny. His lungs felt as if they were on fire.

Sarah shook her head. Her face was red from exertion, making her freckles appear pale. She gasped, "Dixon, I see what you mean about Mergal. Ugh—he looks like somethin' out of a Boris Karloff horror movie!"

A harsh cackling made both of them start. It came from over their heads. A crow had landed high in a nearby maple, its shoulders hunched and its beaky head bobbing. It made a chattery *ka-ka-ka* sound, as if it were laughing scornfully. Goosebumps prickled Johnny's arms.

Was it the same bird that had perched on old Mergal's window? It very well might be.

"Get out of here!" Sarah stooped, picked up a pebble, and with a quick sidearm throw sent it whooshing through the foliage. Five or six leaves came whirling lazily down, but Sarah had missed her target by inches. As she stooped for more ammunition, the crow flapped its wings and took off, and in a moment it was a black speck in the sky above the hilltop. "I think we'd better move along," said Sarah.

They lost no time heading for Fillmore Street. Johnny and Sarah went straight to Professor Childermass' house. Johnny rang the doorbell, but no one answered. That was strange, because the maroon Pontiac was in the garage.

Johnny turned the knob and found the front door was not locked. "I'm going to check this out," he said. He pushed the door open and went inside. "Professor?" he yelled. "Hey, Professor Childermass?"

No one was home. After the warm sun the inside of the old stucco house was cool and dim. They looked in the kitchen. "That's strange," Sarah said. On the kitchen table was a cup half full of black coffee and a plate that held part of a bacon, lettuce, and tomato sandwich.

Johnny touched the cup. "It's cold. What happened to him?"

"This is like that mystery ship. You know, the *Mary Celeste*," Sarah said. Johnny had read the haunting true story of the abandoned ship once, so he knew what she meant. The *Mary Celeste* was a sailing vessel that someone found drifting and deserted back in the nineteenth century. According to the legend, the salvagers who boarded the *Mary Celeste* discovered a half-eaten meal in the galley, but not a living soul was aboard. They towed the ship to port, but no one ever learned what became of the ship's officers and crew. They had all vanished into thin air.

Johnny and Sarah searched the house. Professor Childermass was not home, but they saw no evidence that the burglar had returned. "I don't like this," Johnny said. The two of them went back downstairs. They closed the door behind them and hurried across to Johnny's house.

Gramma Dixon made tomato soup and egg salad sandwiches for lunch, but as she served them, she said she had no idea of where the professor was. "He mighta gone t' visit Dr. Coote," she offered. "I saw Dr. Coote over there a coupla days ago."

After lunch Johnny tried to telephone Dr. Coote, but no one answered. Then he put in a call to the University of New Hampshire, where Dr. Coote taught. A receptionist told him that Dr. Coote was away for a couple of weeks, first to take care of some final details about the publication of his voodoo book and then to fly to England to do some research on medieval magic. Johnny thanked her and hung up.

"Come on," he told Sarah grimly. "I don't like the

professor just disappearing like this, and I know someone who can help us." They went to St. Michael's Church, and Johnny rang the rectory doorbell. At first no one answered, and from inside the house Johnny could hear the sound of a guitar and a strong voice singing the old Irish rebellion song, "The Rising of the Moon." He knocked on the door and the music stopped. A moment later Father Higgins answered the door. He was not in his priestly vestments, but wore green Army fatigue pants and a plaid cotton shirt.

"Well, well," he said. "What brings you two here? You're Sarah Channing, aren't you? I'm glad to welcome your family to the parish."

Sarah grinned self-consciously. "Thank you," she murmured.

Johnny had held in the story as long as he could. He gasped it out in one breath, concluding, "—and now the professor's gone, but his house is unlocked an' there's a cuppa coffee and a sandwich he didn't even finish—"

With a smile, Father Higgins held up his hand. "Easy, easy, John. Maybe this Mr. Mergal is not a very nice man, and maybe he rigged something to scare people away from his house, but he hasn't kidnapped Roderick. It so happens I know Professor Childermass isn't home and I know why. Come in and relax for a moment and I'll tell you."

Father Higgins led them into the stuffy, old-fashioned parlor of the rectory. Curved iron fixtures projected from the walls. They had once been gaslights, but now they were wired for electricity and held small tulip-shaped bulbs under tiny green shades. Religious pictures and a crucifix hung on the walls, and on the mantel was a big black-and-white framed photograph of a much younger Father Higgins and his mother. The air smelled faintly of incense. Beside Father Higgins' armchair rested his battered old guitar.

The priest made Johnny and Sarah sit on the saggy old sofa while he rummaged through some papers on an end table. "Here we are," he said. "This came in the afternoon mail." He passed the paper to Johnny. "You should read it."

It was a badly typed letter done on a faded black ribbon, with lots of strikeovers:

July 25

Dear Father Higgins,

I am taking a short trip, ~~adn~~ and I wanted to let you ~~kon~~ know so you could tell all my friends ~~tht~~ that I am all right. This business about the burglary and the magic hand has upset me, so I am going ~~tot~~ to take the train up to Vermont, get in some fishing and some reflection, and see if I can't calm down. I will see you in a week or so.

The letter was signed "Roderick Childermass" in blue fountain-pen ink. Below that, also in blue ink, was a PS:

"I may not return by Friday, so please make sure the card is delivered."

Johnny looked up from the letter. "This doesn't look like Professor Childermass' way of writing a letter," he objected.

"It looks like his banged-up old Royal typewriter to me," said Father Higgins. "And you know how he tries to type so fast with two fingers that he's always jamming the keys and having to cross out misspellings. Anyway, that's certainly his signature."

Johnny had to admit that was true. Then he asked, "What does this mean about the card?"

Father Higgins took the letter. "That has to do with you, actually. Last Saturday Rod came to see me because he said a very irritating man had moved into town, and he was afraid he would have to do something about it."

Sarah and Johnny exchanged a glance.

Father Higgins must have misunderstood their look. "I don't think the professor was considering lynching anyone or burning down someone's house. Probably he was thinking about having his phone unlisted or something like that. Or maybe he just planned to get out of town to let his famous temper simmer down. Anyway, he left an envelope and asked me to see that you got it before Friday. It's in my study. I'll be right back." He left them alone.

Sarah sighed. "Well, there goes the *Mary Celeste* theory. I had it figured that supernatural forces had kidnapped the professor."

"Maybe not supernatural forces," whispered Johnny.

Frowning, Sarah said, "Oh, come on, Dixon. The prof says that he's off fishing. My dad's like that. Give him half a chance, and he grabs his rods and reels and heads for the nearest damp spot."

Johnny shook his head. "No! Professor Childermass doesn't fish much because he doesn't have the patience. And he wouldn't just take off without letting me know or cleaning up his kitchen. He can be a pretty sloppy housekeeper, but he'd never leave food out to attract bugs."

Father Higgins returned and handed Johnny a square envelope. "Here you are," he said.

Johnny opened the envelope. It held a dime-store birthday card, with a cartoon cake on the front. The colorful cake looked about nine feet tall, and huge red and blue and yellow candles stuck out of it, dripping wax all over.

Inside, the message read: "Here is a BIG CAKE to go with your BIG DAY. Happy birthday!" Beneath that, Professor Childermass had scrawled,

Dear Johnny,

I take this occasion to wish you many happy returns. To make the day fun, I have hidden your present. Here is your clue:

> *Way up high,*
> *An ear in the sky,*
> *A line nearby,*

The package lies
Where billows rise.

I certainly hope I've given you a hand!
Happy birthday!

Always your friend,

Roderick Childermass

Johnny's heart sank. He looked up at the priest.

Father Higgins stared at him. "Why, John! What's wrong?"

In a trembling voice Johnny said, "The professor almost never calls me Johnny. And it isn't my birthday. My birthday's not for months. Oh, Father Higgins, don't you see? The professor's in trouble—terrible, terrible trouble!"

CHAPTER THIRTEEN

They talked to Father Higgins for an hour. The priest knew Johnny was really a level-headed kid, even though he liked to daydream. And he knew that Johnny was serious in his concern for Professor Childermass. However, Father Higgins pointed out, there really was no reason to worry. "He may have been pulling your leg with that card," the priest said. "Or it's even possible there's a secret message in it somehow. But anyway, the professor clearly told me he might not return before Friday. Now, don't you think we should give our friend at least that long? Today's Tuesday. You'll only have to wait three more days. And then, if Rod hasn't called or returned, I promise we'll see if we can get to the bottom of whatever mystery you think you've found."

Johnny wasn't really satisfied with that, but he had to accept it. For a change, Sarah was quiet and shy. In the Catholic school that she had attended before, priests were mysterious and rather ominous characters. They came around to catechize you and to listen to you confess all the bad things you had thought or done.

Johnny and Sarah left the rectory and went their separate ways, but Sarah promised to call him that night. She did, right after dinner. "Listen," she told Johnny, "I've been puzzling over all this. I really don't think we should wait until Friday. Do you?"

"No. By Friday something awful might have happened to the professor. But what can we do?"

"We can keep an eye on old Freak-Face Mergal's house."

"What! After that—that walking skeleton, and the snakes, and—"

"They didn't hurt us, did they? Father Higgins is right. They're something old Mergal fixed up to scare people away. Only we won't be scared! Listen." And Sarah spun out a plan. A plan almost as daredevil and chancy as one of Fergie's. Johnny listened with a strange mixture of dread and excitement. He didn't really want to agree to it, but he was sick and tired of doing nothing. "Okay," he said at last. "Come over early tomorrow, and I'll see you then." He hung up the phone and wondered if he had made a wise decision.

That night as he lay in bed, Johnny studied the birthday card. What did it mean? Was it a cry for help? A warning of danger? Johnny counted the candles. There were twenty-one, seven of each color. The cake had pink, green, and yellow frosting, and the candle flames were yellow with orange centers. Did the candles have a concealed meaning, or the cake? Or did the picture mean anything at all? And what about the puzzling message scrawled inside the card? Johnny read it again. He wondered if the professor's mentioning the word *hand* had any significance. Of course, to say that you'd give someone a hand didn't mean an actual hand—or even a wooden one. And what in the world was an ear high in the sky? Nothing made sense.

Worn out, Johnny laid the card aside, took off his glasses, and clicked off the lamp. Everything that had happened began to whirl around in his head: Miss Ferrington, his job, the delivery man on the loading dock, the snow globe with its frightened little figure, the bizarre wooden hand, and brooding over everything, the terrifying Mr. Mergal. Johnny drifted into a troubled sleep still fretting about all his problems.

Much later he heard a fluttery sound, a stealthy tapping sound. Frowning, he opened his eyes. It was still dark, and the luminous hands of his clock showed the time was five minutes past one. Johnny turned on his side. A pale moon made the window show up as a vague rectangle, a little lighter than the darkness. A shadow flitted over it, and for an instant there was a scratching noise. Johnny slowly reached for his glasses, his heart thumping. He found his spectacles and put them on.

The air had a strange, dusty scent that he could not name. He squinted, staring hard at the window, but nothing moved there.

Johnny eased out of bed and looked outside. A thin mist hung over everything, pale blue with the moonlight. Again Johnny heard a quick, light tapping. Puzzled, he went to the window and pressed his nose against the cool glass, trying to see if some moth or night-flying bird was responsible for the noise. He had a clear view and yet could see nothing. The window was open about six inches. He cautiously raised the sash all the way, feeling the cool rush of night air. Although the tapping sounded again, nothing was visible out there. Still, he leaned over the windowsill to make sure.

With a sudden shock, Johnny saw that the screen was gone. He and Grampa had taken down the storm windows and put up the screens last March. The window was wide open now, with nothing between it and the night—

Invisible hands seized Johnny's shoulders.

Johnny screeched in terror as the hands yanked him out the opening. He clawed desperately for a handhold. "You're comin' with me!" shrieked the voice of Eddie Tompke. "Let's see how far ya can fly!"

Johnny fell headfirst toward the ground twenty feet below—

He hit the floor and thrashed, rocking his night table. The lamp crashed to the floor, and a book he had been reading hit him on the shoulder. Only then did

Johnny realize that he had been having another nightmare.

The door opened and the light snapped on. Standing there in his bathrobe and slippers, his fringe of hair frazzled around his ears, was a startled-looking Grampa Dixon. "Johnny! What in th' world is—"

Johnny pushed up from the floor, and something black jumped off the night table, just above his head. It headed for the dark square of the window, flapping its wings. Johnny screamed as he recognized the malevolent crow, and saw that in its talons the crow was carrying off the card Professor Childermass had left for him. The window was open six inches or so. The bird flattened, sailed into the opening, and with a rattle of cardboard jerked the card through behind it. In a moment the creature had vanished into the night.

Grampa helped Johnny up from a tangle of sheets. "What in th' world was that?" asked the old man. "A bat?"

"A crow," croaked Johnny.

"Did it scare ya? Was that what made the thump?"

Johnny stooped to get his glasses from where they had fallen. "No," he said. "I had a bad dream, but I think the crow might have caused it."

Grampa went to the window and inspected it. "No wonder it could get in so easy. Screen fell right off," he said. "Funny. There hasn't been a storm or anything. Oh, well, I'll take care of it t'morrow." He pulled the window down so it was cracked open only a couple of inches. "I always heard that crows were a thievin' kinda bird, but I never heard of one flyin' right into a house like that. Maybe it was somebody's tame bird and thought this was its home or somethin'. Anyhow, it can't get in now with the window nearly shut. Hope it didn't take anything important. Y' glasses okay?"

Johnny had picked up everything. "Yes," he said in a dull voice.

"Sleep tight, then. Yell if that sneaky old bird comes back."

"Thanks, Grampa," said Johnny.

The old man flicked off the light, closed the door, and left Johnny alone in the dark. Johnny lay awake and thought about what had happened. He was more convinced than ever that the professor was in some awful trouble, and that Mergal was at the root of it. Every time he closed his eyes, he imagined the gaunt, bald Mattheus Mergal leering at him in triumph. Somehow Johnny knew that the evil bird had been sent by the would-be sorcerer, and somehow he knew that the card was already in Mergal's hands. What terrible thing had just happened? Johnny did not know, but he had the dreadful feeling that it might spell death for the professor.

Hours passed with Johnny tossing and turning, trying to get some rest. Finally he drifted to sleep, and this time his dreams were odd but at first not as frightening. He dreamed that he was over at the professor's house and that Professor Childermass was complaining about the Boston Red Sox. "They always leave us in the lurch," the old man growled. "Look at them! At the beginning of June they were in third place! Now they're in fourth, and they're sinking fast toward fifth! Listen to that stupid crowd boo them!"

In the dream, Johnny and the professor were sitting in lawn chairs in the professor's backyard, sipping lemonade under a clear blue summer sky. Johnny said, "I can't hear anything."

"Oh, you can't hear anything with your ear so low. Listen like this!" snapped Professor Childermass. He tilted his head, and his right ear began to grow. It shot way up in the air, on a long thin stalk, until it was higher than the housetop. "Now I can hear them down there in Fenway Park," the professor said. "Oh, no! New York just scored another run! Now the Sox are behind by three. Johnny, you have to give them a hand!"

And the next thing Johnny knew, he was standing at the plate in Fenway Park, the Boston ballpark where the Red Sox played. A New York Yankee pitcher was going into the stretch. Johnny realized he did not have a bat. He looked around frantically for one. A chubby batboy came running over, and with a shock, Johnny saw that the kid had Professor Childermass' face, wire-rimmed spectacles, wild white hair, red strawberry nose and all. "Here you are, slugger," the batboy said, tossing Johnny a light brown bat.

Johnny caught it, and it caught him.

The bat had sprouted a hand. It grasped Johnny's wrist, and he wildly thrashed the bat—

Smack! Completely by accident, the bat connected

with the ball. "Run! Run!" shouted ten thousand people.

Johnny tried to run, but the ball field had turned to sticky mud, and huge clumps of it stuck to his feet. His legs weighed a ton, and he could barely put one foot in front of the other. Each time he did, the foul, thick mud sucked at his shoes, tried to pull him down. And the horrible bat had turned into the wooden hand, its painful grasp tight on his wrist. Johnny was not even halfway to first base, and everything happened in terrible slow motion. A Yankee ballplayer ran toward him, grinning, holding out the ball.

Only it wasn't a ball, but a tiny, bald, pink human head. It had a nasty, evil face, with a long nose, a gash of a mouth, and crooked, stained chattering teeth. Johnny frantically tried to back away, fell, and suddenly went rolling down a steep, steep hill. He woke up with a gasp and a jerk and saw that the window was full of early morning light.

Feeling woozy, Johnny sat on the edge of his bed. He looked out the window at the professor's house, with its ridiculous Italian cupola.

And then Johnny grinned.

His latest nightmare had solved one of his problems. He now knew why the professor had written the strange message on the birthday card. He knew what the ear in the sky was. And he even had a strong suspicion about what he would find in the place where billows rise.

Now all he needed was the courage to go look for it.

) 123 (

CHAPTER FOURTEEN

Johnny slipped across Fillmore Street. It was early—
5:20 A.M., according to his watch—and the street was
deserted. The light fog lingered on, making everything
gray and hazy. So much the better, Johnny thought. If
anyone passed, the chances of his being spotted were that
much less.

He slipped inside the professor's house, but now that
he was actually about to find his "birthday present," he
was frightened. Frightened of where he had to go and
of what he might find.

But he knew he had to go through with it. The professor had risked his life for Johnny more than once. And
so Johnny climbed the stairs to the second floor, then
opened a door at the end of the hallway. It was almost

never used, and its hinges groaned with a high-pitched squeal. The door opened onto a dim stairway that led from the cellar to the unused third floor of the house. Up there, below the roof, were two small servants' rooms and a large, gloomy attic. Johnny climbed up, his breath coming in shallow gasps, the dry dust tickling his nose and making his eyes water.

Both the servants' rooms were empty. A droning fly circled in the warm air and followed Johnny into the large, dark attic. The room was cluttered with boxes, trunks, and old furniture, but there in the center was what Johnny was searching for. It was a cord dangling from the dim ceiling. Johnny found a fairly sturdy chair, pushed it under the cord, and climbed up. He could just reach the wooden bead that hung at the cord's end. Grasping it firmly, Johnny tugged downward.

With a rusty creak, a trapdoor opened overhead and a folding ladder extended itself. Johnny had to move the chair until the ladder was braced, and then he climbed up. Cobwebs swept into his face, making him shiver with revulsion. He climbed up into the dark, yawning rectangle.

At the top he had to crouch, because the trapdoor opened right under the peak of the roof. He felt around on the dry wood, once touching a cold, little many-legged body—a spider! Johnny yanked his hand away. He had heard stories of deadly black widow spiders that could kill a human being with one shot of their lethal venom. Johnny wished that he had thought to bring a flashlight with him, but he had been too excited at the time.

Grimacing, Johnny put his fingertips on the wood again. This time, as if by instinct, he found a rough, rusty metal handle. He gave this a turn, and it ground slowly through half a circle. Then he pushed. A crack of pale, milky daylight showed, and then light flooded in. Johnny had opened a second trapdoor, this one leading out onto the roof of the professor's house. It was set in a little flat-roofed dormer that faced down the roof slope exactly behind the Italian cupola. The professor had squeezed in and out of this opening many times when he was putting up his homemade radio aerial, because the old man hated heights and ladders. Now Johnny crept cautiously through.

The roof swept dizzily down, and from here Johnny could see the backyard with its incinerator, barbecue grill, and weedy flower beds. Over to his right was the roof of the garage, and through the trees at the back of the yard Johnny glimpsed the alley that ran behind the houses on this side of the street. Everything beyond that was lost in the morning mist. Johnny flattened himself until he was almost lying on the roof and then crawled up to the peak, carefully. Very, very carefully, because he could imagine rolling helplessly down and plummeting to the earth, possibly breaking his neck.

He sat astride the roof like a cowboy on a horse, leaning against the cupola. The ramshackle radio aerial towered over him. Despite his fear, Johnny smiled. This was the ear in the sky. Professor Childermass had built the aerial so he could hear the Red Sox games on his radio. Leading from the aerial, tacked down to the roof and disappearing over the edge, was the antenna wire. And running along beside it, white and almost brand-new, was a length of cotton cord, like clothesline. It ran to the edge of the roof, but then instead of vanishing downward, it led up the chimney side.

The present would be where billows rose—billows of smoke.

Johnny found the end of the cord and tugged. The professor had stapled it down only lightly, and it came loose with a pop. Johnny pulled harder until finally the cord was free of the roof and made a straight line between his hand and the chimney top. Something scraped inside the chimney, and then an oblong package wrapped in soot-blackened cloth came out. It thudded to the roof and rolled a little way before the cord stopped it. Johnny hauled in his catch. It had to be the wooden hand. He wrapped the free part of the cord around and around it, carefully eased down the roof, and scuttled back into the attic. He started to pull the door closed and froze.

A dark shadow zoomed past, disappearing into the fog. Was it a crow?

Johnny couldn't be sure, but he slammed the trapdoor, clambered down the ladder, and sent the folding ladder clashing back up into the ceiling. Then he hurried downstairs. The moment he opened the front door, he saw Sarah pedaling her bike up the street. Johnny dashed out and waved at her. She swerved, and they met at the edge of the professor's driveway.

"Hi," she said. "Whatcha got?"

"My birthday present," Johnny returned, making a face. "Come on and we'll open it."

It was not yet six o'clock, and Gramma and Grampa were still asleep. While Sarah waited in the parlor, Johnny went quietly up to the bathroom, scrubbed his sooty hands and dusty face, and changed clothes. He hurried downstairs and led Sarah into the cellar. "Nobody will come down here," he whispered. "And I don't think any birds can spy on us here either." He hastily told Sarah about how he had solved the professor's puzzle and retrieved the package.

He used his Boy Scout knife to cut the cord that bound the sooty package and then unrolled the old sheet. Inside was the carved wooden hand. Sarah picked it up. "So this is the big deal? What's it supposed to do?"

Johnny shrugged helplessly. "I don't know. It was the last thing that Esdrias Blackleach made before he died. When I first touched it, it—I thought it moved. But Professor Childermass didn't know about any magical powers that it might have, unless Dr. Coote found something."

Sarah grinned. "We can find out. His door's not even locked."

"That seems wrong," said Johnny. "It's like stealing or something."

Sarah began to wrap the hand up again. "What are

you talking about? You've already been in his house once today!"

"That was different. Professor Childermass left the card for me, so he wanted me to find this hand if he couldn't get to it. He didn't tell me just to come into his house and make myself at home."

"How else are we gonna find out what he dug up on old Blackleach?"

Johnny had no answer. They slipped into the professor's house. Johnny led the way up to the cluttered study. A few books were piled on the desk, and some of them obviously had to do with magic. There was the two-volume set of Charles W. Upham's *Salem Witchcraft*, John Hale's *A Modest Enquiry into the Nature of Witchcraft*, Cotton Mather's *Wonders of the Invisible World*, and W. Elliot Woodward's *Records of Salem Witchcraft*. The two friends looked through the indexes, but only two of the books mentioned Blackleach.

Sarah restacked the books, making a face. "Well, that tells us nothing," she grumbled. "Where else would he keep books and stuff?"

They searched through the brick-and-board bookshelves with no luck. Irritated, Sarah scuffed her toe through the ankle-deep pile of old graded exams—and turned up a heavy, crumbling volume that had been thrust underneath them. "Hey," she said. "Here's something." She picked it up. It was a thin, tall book, a folio volume, bound in ancient, flaking leather. The cover no longer bore any title that could be read.

They plopped the book on the desk and Johnny carefully opened it, releasing a cloud of spicy-smelling dust. "It's a holograph," he said.

"A *what?*" demanded Sarah, craning to see.

"A holograph," repeated Johnny. "A book that wasn't printed, but written in longhand." He pointed to the title page, where a spidery title had been written in ink faded to a rusty brown:

A True Relation
of the
Witchcraft Tryals
in New-England

Sarah wrinkled her nose. "The penmanship's awful."

"It's just old-fashioned," returned Johnny. "Hey, here's a bookmark." He opened the book to the place marked by a three- by five-inch note card, and they saw writing on the card. Johnny immediately recognized Dr. Coote's fussy, neat handwriting: "Dear Roderick— I borrowed this monograph from a good friend of mine, so please take care of it. It is the only one in existence, and it may tell you more about your wizard than you want to know." It was signed, "Charles."

Johnny read the faded words on the brittle, ancient page:

Mr. E. B. of Squampatanong Village, a prosperous Farmer, but withal a learned Man, did advise the Magistrates of the divers Means of discovering Witches. Mr. Hathorne did say, that without the Aid of Mr. E. B., the Tryals would not have been Half so successful, nor the Convictions for this Horrid Art or Science of Witch-Craft half so Many.

I watch'd and long wonder'd at this Prodigy, and began to fear that he was not, as he seem'd, a modest helpful Man, but perhaps himself an Instrument of Evil, for to be sure he oft succeeded to the Property of those accused or condemn'd. Mr. E. B. suffer'd a Stroke of Apoplexy in July, and linger'd on most grievously Ill until August, when, on the first Day of the Month, he deliver'd up his Soul. The Skies were rent with Lightning and Thunder, and some Relations of those accus'd, were so Bold as to say that the Devil had come for his Own. Yet the Magistrates held that Practicers of the Wicked Arts rais'd the Storm, to trouble the Last Moments on Earth of a good and godly Soul.

The old man's mutilated Body the Family buried, but in dying, Mr. E. B. left behind him many curious and strange Works, that I acquir'd from his only Son. Among these were a Mirror for sending of Spirits, and a tablet for finding Treasures hid under ground, and a tube of spying from a Distance or at Night, and a Hand marvelously carven of Wood like unto his own, which he lost, and a curious bottle, wherein it snowed, and many Phials of Medicines and Powders besides. All these I have put by, for I am persuaded that E. B. was of the Evil One's Party himself, for he kept the Trappings of the Necromancer's Art.

Sarah pointed to the name. "Mr. E. B. could be Esdrias Blackleach. What does 'mutilated Body' mean?"

Johnny shrugged. "I don't know. But it also says the wooden hand was like the one that E. B. lost. Maybe he had his hand cut off in a farm accident. Anyway, it has to be the same guy." He read more, but the rest of the book talked about the executions in Salem Village, about the oratory of Cotton Mather, and about the villagers' apologies to the surviving accused witches some ten years after the trials had ended. He closed the book and puffed out his breath. "So that's how the hand and the other things came to be preserved," he said. "I suppose whoever wrote this book kept them, and then his heirs got them, and little by little they were scattered until the professor's brother began buying them as antiques."

"But what does Spooky-Face Mergal want with the junk?"

"I told you," said Johnny impatiently. "He thinks he can be a wizard like Blackleach."

Sarah had opened the book back to the marked page. "What in the world is a n-necromancer?" she asked.

"A magician of some kind," Johnny said. "I saw a dictionary of magic over on one of the bookshelves. Let's look it up."

They thumbed through the heavy dictionary until they found the entry. A hideous woodcut illustrated it, showing two men in Elizabethan clothes standing in a magic circle drawn on the soil of a cemetery. A grave yawned open nearby, and standing stiff as a board was a ghastly figure, a dead woman with a skeletal face and a gaping mouth. The caption read, "Dr. Dee and his assistant Kelley performing an act of necromancy."

Johnny's throat felt dry as he read the definition opposite the illustration. "It says here that a necromancer is a magician who has the power to make people rise from the dead."

For a moment the two friends stared wide-eyed at each other. Then the telephone rang, its bell terribly loud in the silent house.

Johnny and Sarah both screamed in alarm.

CHAPTER FIFTEEN

"Sh-should we answer that?" stammered Sarah.

Johnny realized that if the caller were one of the professor's friends, then his presence in the house would be no surprise. He picked up the receiver and held it to his ear without saying anything.

"Hello? Is anyone there?" asked a cranky voice.

Johnny almost burst with relief. "Professor Childermass! We were worried sick about you. Where on earth did you go?"

"Ah, my young friend. Where did I go? Well, here and there, let us say. Did you enjoy your birthday, John?"

Frowning, Johnny realized that something was wrong. The voice *sounded* like the professor's—but it had a kind of false note too. "Uh, yeah," Johnny said. "Thanks for the card, but I—I lost it, an' I don't remember the puzzle. Where did you hide my present, anyway?"

The voice at the other end sighed. "Well, we'll soon deal with that, my boy. In fact, I'm on my way home now. I have decided to sell that carved hand to Mr. Mergal. He seems to be a harmless collector of antiques. So you just wait right there, and we'll find your present together, hmm?"

"O-okay," said Johnny. His face felt numb. He hung up the phone and stared wildly at Sarah. "That was Mergal," he said. "He pretended to be the professor, an' he sounded a lot like him, but it must have been Mergal. He has a little habit of saying, 'hmm' every so often, an' the professor never does that. He's on his way here!"

"Come on!" Johnny followed Sarah downstairs. They went out through the kitchen door and then through the backyard and into the alley. "You see what this means, don't you?"

"What?" Johnny asked.

"Well, if Mergal's gonna be coming here, then he won't be at home. And while he's out, we have to take a look inside that creepy old house of his—because he just may be holding the professor prisoner!"

"Couldn't we call the police or something?" groaned Johnny.

Sarah gave him an exasperated look. "An' tell them what? That we *think* this new guy in town *might* have busted into the museum and *may* have kidnapped the prof, all because he *possibly* wants to be a super-duper necromancer? They'd haul us off to the funny farm!" She punched his arm. "C'mon, Dixon. There's two of us, so one can keep watch while the other explores."

Johnny felt his heart sink, but he had to admit Sarah was right. They made the trek over to Saltonstall Street and cut through a couple of empty lots. These were overgrown with weeds and brushy saplings, so Johnny and Sarah could hide and keep the house in sight. At first they thought Mr. Mergal might already have left, because everything looked so empty and quiet. Then Sarah grabbed Johnny's wrist. A pink blur had appeared at the window in the octagonal tower room. It was Mergal's bald head, peering out suspiciously. It vanished into the gloom, and a few minutes later they heard a car engine cough to life. From somewhere behind the house a shiny black Hudson Hornet came bumping over a rutted drive. It stopped at the wrought-iron fence, and Mergal got out. He glanced all around, opened the gate, climbed back into his automobile, and drove off.

"I'll go," said Sarah. She pulled something from her jeans pocket. It was a shiny silver whistle. "If the car comes back, give a couple of toots. And you listen for me, because if a skeleton comes walking toward me, I'm gonna scream my lungs out!"

"No," said Johnny slowly. "You keep watch. The professor's my friend. I should be the one who goes to look for him."

Sarah turned her surprised, freckled face toward him.

After a moment she grinned. "You're all right, Dixon. Okay, go ahead. Keep an ear peeled for this whistle. If Murderous Mergie shows his nasty face, I'll give you three loud blasts. I mean *loud*!"

Johnny trotted across the street. The mist had burned off, but the day was gloomy and overcast. He had the same oppressive feeling as before that the weathered old gray house was watching him, like some evil predator. He hurried to the gate that Mergal had left open and rushed up to a side door. Locked. He went around back, tried what must have been the kitchen door, and had better luck. It opened, yawning into darkness.

Johnny stepped across the threshold, his heart in his mouth. He was in a sparsely furnished kitchen. A scarred wooden table dominated the center of the room, cluttered with newspapers and dirty cups. A junky old gas range and a refrigerator stood against the wall opposite the door, and to Johnny's left was a rust-streaked sink piled high with dirty dishes. The faucet dripped, making a dismal "thunk . . . thunk" sound like a slow heartbeat. The air smelled stale and sour, with a sweetish, disgusting undertone of old garbage.

"Professor?" Johnny called. No one answered.

The adjoining room was a bedroom, with Mergal's clothes in the closet and the bed unmade. The other rooms on the first floor were empty except for dust and slowly swaying cobwebs. He looked out the front window and spotted Sarah only because he knew just where to look. He rapped on the window and she waved at him in a hurry-up-why-don't-you way. With his footsteps sounding hollow in the empty rooms, Johnny explored further.

The second floor was empty, like the front rooms downstairs. What Johnny thought at first to be a closet proved to be a doorway to a spiral staircase leading up into gloom. Biting his lip, Johnny tiptoed up. They had seen Mergal in the tower, and that could be where he had stashed the professor. The air was suffocating, and Johnny was sweating heavily.

He reached the top of the stairs and cautiously opened the door he found there. He stepped out into an octagonal room, with a round window in each wall, all but one covered by green shades. The roof slanted up, the exposed beams rising to the center. Unlike the deserted chambers below, this room was crammed with tables, shelves, and boxes.

Johnny closed the door and felt his heart thumping painfully. A rectangular table stood in the middle of the room, and on the floor around it was a double circle painted in white. The inner circle contained a five-pointed star, so big that the table stood in the center without touching any line. The space between the inner and outer circles contained lettering like hen scratches. Johnny had seen the figure in books on sorcery. It was a pentacle, a magic circle drawn to protect a wizard or a witch from the wrath of any demons that he or she might summon up. According to legend, evil forces could not pass beyond the unbroken perimeter of such a shield.

And the table in the center was a witch's altar. On it two brass candlesticks held partly burned black candles. A long stick lay across the table, and Johnny wondered if that was the staff Mergal had used to conjure up the Independence Day storm. A brass incense burner, a dagger, and an ominous black-bound book also rested on the table. For some reason Johnny did not care to step inside the magic circle. He edged around it, toward a bricked-up fireplace, because on the mantel he had noticed some familiar objects.

He caught his breath. Sure enough, the mantel held a wooden-framed hand mirror, its silver backing long tarnished away and its glass an oval of darkness. Next to it was an ornate little wooden snuffbox with the head of a goat carved into its lid. Just beyond that was a short stack of ancient books. On top of the books was a greenish snow dome with a flattened top. Johnny had discovered the missing items from the museum, the lost possessions of old Esdrias Blackleach, wizard.

Johnny realized that at last he had something solid. Maybe he hadn't found Professor Childermass, but this was almost as good. If the police arrested Mergal for stealing all this stuff from the museum, then they could surely persuade him to tell them what he had done with the professor. Still, he had to have some real proof—

A shrill sound startled him. Was it the whistle? He ran

to the front window, but dust clouded it so he could not see clearly. He found a catch and pushed, and the window swiveled out. Johnny stretched his neck to peer out of the window, and far below he could see Sarah's red T-shirt. She crouched in the brush with her elbows on her knees, resting her chin in both hands. Obviously she had not blown the whistle. Johnny thought he was probably just jumpy, and that he had imagined the sound. Still, now that he had found something, he needed to get out of there fast—but not without proof.

The snow globe would do. He went back to the mantel and picked it up. It was the museum's, all right, because Johnny could see the little crack he had made when he had bumped it to the floor. Evidently the flaw went all the way through, because a small air bubble now bobbed at the top of the globe. The water was slowly evaporating. He turned it over and saw scratched into the ash-wood base the name *Esdrias Blackleach* and the date *Feb 1690*.

As Johnny moved, he turned the globe over and the snow inside it swirled into a miniature blizzard. Johnny's ears began to buzz strangely, and he felt dizzy, as if he had turned in rapid circles and had suddenly come to a stop. He blinked and focused his eyes on the figure in the snow globe, forever striding toward the safety of the cabin and forever failing to reach it. The flakes flew around the lonely traveler, swooping and spiraling. It was getting hard to breathe, and the air felt wrong, thick and heavy. Outside the window a noisy crow was screeching *graaa! graaa! graaa!* over and over.

No. It was a higher-pitched sound, not a bird at all, but—a whistle!

Johnny gasped. He realized that he had been standing there hypnotized by the globe for a long time, ten or fifteen minutes maybe. The whistle shrilled again. He ran across the outer edge of the pentacle, not bothering to duck around it, and flung open the door.

Something pale and round was coming up the stairway, and in it two deep-set eyes burned. It was Mergal's bald head and face, almost glowing in the gloom. Johnny retreated, the snow globe clutched against his chest.

"Ah, my good friend from the museum," Mergal said as he stepped into the room. He wore a completely black outfit—black shoes, trousers, coat, and shirt. His pale face and hands floated, almost disconnected from his body in the dim light of the octagonal room. The hoarse voice droned on: "But we've met since then, have we not? In your dreams, hmm? Or in your nightmares?"

Johnny blinked at him. "N-nightmares?" he heard himself squeak.

The brown-toothed smile twisted itself across the man's cruel face. "Yes, I sent you a few gentle reproofs. After all, you were not very helpful at our first meeting, hmm? Nor was your friend, the stuffy old professor. I threw a few bolts of, ah, divine fire at the old man to punish him for *his* attitude. You were quite nearby, as I recall, too close for comfort, in fact. You have my property there. I will trouble you to hand it over."

Johnny's knees were shaking. The whistle had fallen silent. Had Sarah gone for help? Or had something happened to her? Stalling for time, Johnny said, "It isn't yours. It belongs to the professor."

"Alas, you are mistaken. All these implements, and more besides, are heirlooms passed down to me from my illustrious ancestor, Esdrias Blackleach. What would our mutual friend the professor call him?" Mergal paused, his head tilted as if he were listening. When he spoke again, his voice was so exactly like Professor Childermass' that it sent chills down Johnny's spine: "Why, the man was nothing more than a posturing charlatan, a brass-bound, copper-bottomed fake. And I can spot a phony a mile away."

"It *was* you on the phone," said Johnny. "And you wrote that note to Father Higgins too, an' made the professor sign it, didn't you?"

"Let us say that I *persuaded* the old man to sign it. And the fool tried to trick me by sneaking in a message to you. Much good it did him! Your friend is now my guest, as indeed are you. However, it would be most awkward to have the two of you together at present. After all, the old windbag has yet to surrender the most important part of my property. And speaking of my property, give me my globe, boy!"

The man's eyes had been staring into Johnny's, and the whipcrack of the last three words came so suddenly that Johnny handed the globe over without thinking. Mergal took it in his long, crooked fingers. "Very good, child. You are learning obedience. I could destroy you and reduce your brain to ashes. Or I could transform you into something that people would kill on sight. It might be amusing to send you blundering and mewling into your dear grandparents' home late at night. Does your grandfather keep a loaded gun in the house, boy, hmm? Or I could simply drive you insane. But no, I think not yet. I may have a use for you."

Johnny swayed. The hoarse, quiet words struck terror deep into the marrow of his bones, but he could not break the spell. He could not bring himself to look away from those burning eyes.

With his twisted smile, Mergal softly continued: "That foolish professor will change his tune when he knows you are at my mercy. However, I can't be seen with you in public, and I can't run the risk of your fleeing. I need some, ah, container, some handy place of imprisonment. Fortunately this globe has a sweet little spell attached to it. I may as well try it on you."

He held the globe up so that his eyes peered into Johnny's over the top of the glass, and slowly he began to swirl the snow inside. It spun in a miniature whirlwind, faster and faster. "Just keep looking," Mergal crooned, "and I will show you a great wonder." He began to chant in a flat, high-pitched tone, and the words he spoke were foreign, uncanny.

Johnny's head swam. Everything grew dark, until there were only the two burning eyes and the swirling white cone of snow. Then even they faded out. The air was heavy, and Johnny's chest labored to pump it into his lungs. The darkness slowly became milky-white, like a fog with the sun shining through it. The door was just in front of him. Johnny stretched out his hand for the knob and closed his fist on empty air.

He took a shuffling step forward, then tried again. The doorknob was not real, but only a painting of a doorknob. He turned and tried to see the windows, but that milky light concealed everything. Johnny staggered a few steps, his feet like lumps of lead. He limped in half a circle, then turned back. Far away was a log cabin, small and dark among the faded green fir trees. Something pale and shining was rising behind it, a monster moon that filled the whole sky.

No. It was not the moon, for within it were two fierce eyes. It was the face of Mattheus Mergal, swollen to incredible vastness. The twisted brown grin leered at him. "One swirl brings pain," the man's awful voice rasped. "Two bring agony. And I'm afraid the third storm is death, my intruding young friend. Let's try the first, shall we? Hmm?"

The whole world revolved, and huge white flakes filled the air. They touched Johnny's face and hands, and he yelped, for they were so terribly cold they burned like red-hot knives stripping away his skin. He ran blindly, smashing against an invisible wall that was hard and unyielding.

He screamed, and his voice was thin and stretched, like the whine of a mosquito. Somehow Mergal had trapped him, had worked an awful spell.

Johnny had become the figure inside the snow globe.

CHAPTER SIXTEEN

"Ah," rumbled the terrible voice of the giant Mergal. "You realize, I see, what you have become. Realize too, boy, that you are no more than an insect to me, no more than an annoyance. Now that I have you prisoner, I must see to my other, ah, guest. The time is far too near for my plans to be thwarted by such meddling nonentities, hmm?"

The world reeled as Mergal placed the snow globe down on the table inside the magic circles. Johnny stumbled and thrashed. The "snow" was more than ankle deep, and it froze his feet with a burning cold. He staggered to the stand of conical fir trees. The glass curved under at the edges, with the wooden base cemented to it below. He stepped onto the glassy margin and found it was slippery as ice. He thrust out his tiny hands and leaned against the transparent wall. It occurred to Johnny that he was breathing water, and the idea panicked him, but in the grotesque world inside the snow globe, the water seemed to serve just as well as air.

Now the glass walls of the globe seemed immensely thick to him, and the greenish glass distorted his view. Mergal was at the mantel, busily picking up the other witch relics and tucking them into a wicker basket. Johnny realized that the man was packing, as if for a trip. Undoubtedly he meant to force Professor Childermass to reveal the secret hiding place of the wooden hand. What would happen when he discovered the hand had been taken away?

Mergal turned and strode over to the table. He leaned close, his ghastly grin bigger than a house, and Johnny stumbled backward. He heard Mergal's thunderous laughter. "No doubt you are wondering why I am gathering the legacy of my illustrious ancestor. Well, there's no reason why I shouldn't tell you the truth: I intend to raise the spirit of Esdrias Blackleach from the dead! With the help of the necromantic hand, I will invite his spirit, with all its knowledge of sorcery, to inhabit my body, sharing it with my own soul. Together we will be invincible. Unfortunate Esdrias! He was ambitious, but he lived in a poor, petty time, and his ambitions were poor and petty. With me to serve as his host and show him the way, and him to provide the magical know-how, we two will rule the world!"

Johnny clapped his hands over his ears. Mergal's hideous laughter was so loud that it was painful. He saw Mergal stride out the staircase door. Johnny was alone in the dreadful trap of the snow globe.

His first thought was that he would freeze. The snow might not be real to anyone else, but to the figure inside the globe it was obviously deadly. Johnny floundered to the log cabin and tried to find some way of getting inside. Surely if Mergal intended the globe to be a prison and not a death trap, the cabin would offer some protection.

Johnny was disappointed. The cabin was one block of wood, just shaped and painted to resemble a house. Maybe Mergal didn't realize how cold it was inside the globe, how the snow slowed his footsteps and chilled his blood and made him sleepy. . . .

With a start Johnny jerked awake. He had sunk to his knees and had almost passed out. Johnny had read of the deadly sleep that sometimes overtook Arctic explorers. He had to keep moving, and he had to try to keep warm. He went to the edge of the snow again and prowled the perimeter of the globe, staring out into the room. He stopped and gasped. Through the thick green glass he could see a still, distorted figure lying on the floor just outside the magic circle. It wore glasses, a dark blue shirt, blue jeans, and sneakers. The figure was Johnny himself.

His head spun. How could he be inside the globe and yet outside on the floor at the same time? It was impossible. He felt like sobbing from terror and despair, but he forced himself to try to think his way through this problem. *It has to be a hallucination*, he told himself. *Somehow, Mergal is making me think I'm inside the snow globe when I'm really out there, unconscious.* That made sense, in a bizarre kind of way, but it did Johnny absolutely no good. After all, if the hallucination seemed as real as this to him, it would either kill him or drive him permanently insane. Maybe he could convince himself that the experience was not real, maybe he could force himself to wake up outside of the globe, safe and sound.

He stooped and picked up a chunk of the snow. He didn't know what it was—something white and glittery. *This isn't real snow*, he told himself. *It isn't really cold. It can't hurt me or—*

It was no use. The enormous snowflake numbed his hands. He dropped it, and it fluttered down like a falling leaf. The power of the evil wizard was greater than Johnny's ability to reason away the magic.

A movement caught his eye. The door was opening again. Something red was coming into the room—

Sarah! She had followed him into the house!

Johnny ran to the edge of the glass and beat on it as he yelled. Sarah did not notice him. She ran to the fallen figure of Johnny on the floor and stooped over him. Then she grabbed both of his feet and began to tug. She was going to try to pull him out through the staircase. Johnny winced. Didn't she know that if she dragged him downstairs his head would bang against each step on the way down? He'd get a concussion, or he might even be killed.

Then he remembered the crack in the glass globe that he had accidentally made. If he could find that, maybe he could break the dome. He had a confused notion that the magic would all leak out with the water, and maybe that would free him.

He ran around the globe until he saw it. When Johnny was his normal size, the crack was just a hairline flaw, barely visible in good light. Now, though, it was a jagged crevice. Johnny felt in his pockets. He had his Boy Scout knife. He took it out, opened the longest blade, and began to chip at the edge of the crack. Little flakes of glass flew, like pieces of ice. It was slow going. Compared to his present size, the glass was a foot thick. It would take forever.

He saw Sarah slowly pulling his body along by the ankles. His arms—his real arms—had gone out to the sides. Watching the scene, Johnny missed a blow with the knife, and his knuckles crashed against the broken edge of the glass. Pain flashed through his whole arm, and a swirl of red blood flew from the cut. "Ahh!" Johnny yanked his hand away, dropping the knife.

Outside the globe, Johnny suddenly jerked his real right hand. It hit an unsteady leg of the magic altar, and the table toppled away from the figure on the floor. The snow globe, already close to the edge, slid off. Inside the globe, Johnny saw the deadly snow swirling. He fell to his knees and crumpled to the ground—

Crash! With a shock like an electrical jolt, a bright flash of light exploded. Everything whirled, went black, and then his ears filled with a high, humming sound. He struggled to open his eyes—

And looked up at Sarah. *"Aawwhhk,"* he wheezed. He was freezing.

She dropped his feet, with a look of frantic relief. "C'mon, we gotta get out of here before Baldy Buzzard gets back. What did he do to you, anyway? Give you some kind of voodoo drug or something?"

Johnny could not stop shaking. He rolled over, got to his knees, and hugged himself. He felt as if the air in the room were fifty degrees below zero. His right hand throbbed with pain, although he could see no trace of a wound. He blinked at the floor. The snow globe was in a thousand pieces. Water pooled beneath it, and the little wooden figure lay face down in the corner of the room. Johnny was finally free, but the effects of the spell still lingered and almost paralyzed him.

Sarah helped him up. Together they stumbled down the spiral staircase. He kept blacking out and pausing, but Sarah urged him on. They got to the first floor and headed for the kitchen. Johnny could move a little better now. His legs worked again, and the feeling of numbing cold was passing off with a pins-and-needles prickling.

Sarah opened the door a crack, peered out, and then led the way into the backyard. "Good thing for you old Mergal came in the front. I found this way in and explored until I discovered the staircase. What happened, anyway?"

"Not now," Johnny gasped. "Tell you later."

They had taken no more than a couple of steps away from the house when a black bird fluttered to a limb of the dead elm tree. It gave them a beady red stare, threw back its head, and shouted out a raucous "*Caw!*"

"The crow!" Johnny panted. "A familiar of—of old Mergal."

Sarah knew that a familiar was an animal or bird that a wizard had enchanted, or sometimes it was an evil spirit in the shape of an animal or a bird. Familiars served as spies and servants for witches and sorcerers. She picked up a rock and threw it hard. The stone was right on target, and with a final harsh screech, the crow *exploded* into a puff of feathers and smoke. Even the feathers dissolved as they floated down toward the ground. Sarah was shaking. "I g-guess I owe you an apology, Dixon," she muttered. "Th-that wasn't a real bird at all—"

Johnny nodded. The day was getting darker, with low, ugly, hanging gray clouds. "We g-gotta find out wh-where M-m-m—" stammered Johnny, his teeth still chattering.

"I know where Mergal's gone," Sarah said. "He's next door!"

Johnny gave her a wild look. "Y-you mean the old—"

"The old church," Sarah finished for him. "I saw him slip into a side door. Come on!" At the edge of the yard, she reached under a bush and dragged out the wrapped-up hand. "I don't suppose you found out what Mergal wants with this," she said.

"H-he wants to use it to raise old Esdrias Blackleach from the dead."

Sarah stared at him. "No kidding?"

"No kidding."

They hid in the vacant lot again, crouched under some bushes. After ten long minutes Mergal emerged from a side door of the old burned-out church, gazed up in the air as if he were uneasy, and locked the door behind him. He strode to his house, went to the front door, and disappeared inside.

Sarah and Johnny edged around until the church was between them and the house. Then they dashed across the street. The sanctuary of the church was too choked with debris and ashes to let them get in that way, and the undamaged part of the building had no door on this side. However, some frosted-glass windows, most of them cracked, still were in place, evidently leading down into a basement. Sarah found another rock and bashed it through the glass. Then she reached in, unlocked the window frame, and pushed it open. "Let's go," she said grimly. She rolled onto her stomach and wormed backward through the opening.

Johnny followed. They were in a room that might have been where choir robes and hymnals were stored. At the far end was a flight of steps leading up, and on either side were doors. One of them had a shiny new padlock on it.

"That's it," Sarah said. She ran to the door and pounded on it. "Anybody there?"

Something rustled inside, and a hoarse voice called, "Who's that?"

"Professor!" Johnny yelled. "We came to rescue you. Wait a minute and we'll have you out!" In the dimness the door looked solid, but it had one weakness: It opened outward. The hinges were on the outside.

Johnny dragged an old chair from what must have once been a Sunday-school room and stood on it. He opened his knife, slipped the blade beneath the head of the top hinge pin, and pried it up. The pin slipped upward slowly, until it flew out and clattered on the floor. Johnny jumped off the chair and went to work on the middle hinge. Soon he had it loose too. Then the bottom one. As soon as the last hinge pin fell free, Johnny jumped back and said, "Push the door, Professor!"

The door swiveled out, held only by the lock. Professor Childermass stumbled forward. He looked terrible. His hair was unkempt and tangled, and white stubble glittered on his chin. Johnny hugged him anyway.

"Quick," Sarah said. "Mergal's probably on his way here right now."

"I solved the riddle," Johnny babbled. "We brought the hand, and—"

"What!" said the professor. "You brought the hand with you? Give it to me at once!"

Sarah handed the wrapped bundle to the professor, saying, "We think Mergal's up to something awful."

"He sure is," the professor said gravely, unwrapping the hand and letting the cloth fall to the floor. "He won't be able to do a thing, though, if we can destroy this cursed relic. Let's go." He staggered. "Sorry," he mumbled. "Been without food for a couple of days. I'm afraid you'll have to help me."

He leaned on Johnny, and the two of them followed Sarah up the staircase. At the top they found themselves in a maddening little maze of small windowless rooms. Finally they found a hallway, with an arched door at the end. They hurried toward it.

It boomed open.

Mattheus Mergal stood there, his staff in his right hand, and his face writhing with anger.

"Well, how convenient," he said in a nasty voice. "All the little birdies together, hmm? And now we'll be more cooperative, won't we, Professor? Unless we want to see our friends' eyes plucked out and tossed to my little pet?"

A black form fluttered up and landed on his shoulder. It was the crow, or another one just like it, and its beak clacked greedily, as if it understood the ghastly offer its master had just made.

"I've finished playing with you!" Mergal shouted. "Now, all of you worms will understand the wrath of a warlock!" He pointed the staff at the frightened trio and began to speak short words, sharp as shattered glass, bitter as death.

CHAPTER SEVENTEEN

"Wait!" said Professor Childermass in his weak voice. "Let these children go free, and I will give you what you want."

Mergal paused. He lowered the staff. "Prove it," he said. "Show me that you know what I desire, and I will consider your offer."

Professor Childermass cleared his throat. "You are seeking a relic of Esdrias Blackleach," he said, "a carving in the shape of a left hand, done in ash wood."

Mergal's deep-set eyes flared, and his brown teeth showed in a sharklike grin. "And you know where this artifact is, hmm? Just as I suspected. Oh, you were stubborn, old man! But now you will tell me."

"Only if you let John and Sarah go free."

The brown grin became even more unpleasant. "No, no, my friend. You have it backward. You will tell me where you hid the hand, and then, if I recover it, I may let your young friends off easily. Of course, you will still have to suffer for being so haughty and proud. You never expected to get away unpunished, did you, hmm?"

"We appear to be at a stalemate," the professor said. "I assure you, if you so much as touch either of these two young people, you will never know where the hand is hidden. And if I possibly can, I'll destroy the wretched thing, or have someone else destroy it."

Mergal actually snarled, like an animal. "Fool! You do not understand its great potency! If you should even crack its little finger—" Mergal broke off. His grin came back. "Ah, clever, aren't we, hmm? Tried to trick the stupid old wizard, didn't we? The game isn't that easy, my friend!"

Johnny stood behind the professor. When the door of the church first opened, Professor Childermass had quickly tucked the hand into the waistband of his trousers, against his spine. Its fingers stuck out now, waving. Mergal glared at Johnny. "There's one score the boy and I must settle. He destroyed something of mine! I don't know how the brat did it, but he broke a very pretty spell. I felt some of my power go with it. To get it back I will have to perform a blood sacrifice."

The professor crossed his arms. "We won't get anywhere like that," he said. "Tell me, Mergal, what do you propose to do with this blasted wooden hand, anyway?

Are you going to chop down a tree and carve a one-handed department-store dummy to go with it?"

Mergal pushed the heavy door behind him, and it swung closed with a dull thud. "Ah, well, it wouldn't interest a scholar, the story of our humble experiments in the mystic arts. People don't believe in magic anymore, hmm?" He tried a smile like a horrible simper. He looked like the world's oldest baby trying to trick his mother into giving him a cookie. "But, the hand is, ah, a requirement for some astrological studies. Yes, yes, that's it. The hand will enable me to forecast the future accurately. To see what stocks are going up, and what stocks are going down—"

"Watch it, Professor!" Johnny yelled. "He's usin' his voice to try to hypnotize you! He did it to me back in his house!"

Mergal snarled. "Perhaps I shall take a large darning needle and sew your tongue between your lips. That would teach you not to interrupt!"

"Forget it, Mergal," the professor said. His right hand eased behind him, close to the wooden wrist jammed under his belt. "You were lying, anyway. The hand has nothing to do with astrology."

Mergal snorted. "I suppose you know better."

"I know a little about magic," the professor said. "I know, for instance, about the Hand of Glory. That's the severed hand of a hanged man, dried and treated with oils. If you have one, you light the fingers like candles. As long as they are burning, you can creep into anyone's house without waking the occupants. It seems to me that such a thing would be ideal for a sneak thief like you!"

The man in black had crept to within a few feet of the others. He snickered, an unpleasant sound. "You're completely wrong," he said. "Yes, there is such a thing as the Hand of Glory, but the Blackleach hand is altogether different. Different and more powerful, hmm?"

"Yes," the professor said. "Maybe it doesn't put people in a trance at all. Maybe it opens a gate."

Mergal's face contorted. "How much do you know?" he rasped. Then his jaw became set and grim. "No matter. I can see there is no dealing with you. I shall have to use my powers to impress you, hmm? You want out of this place, don't you? In a minute you shall be quite free to leave—if you dare!" He spoke more words, raised the staff in his hand, and brought it whistling down. It struck the floor of the church with a loud rap.

"Listen," Mergal said with a grin. "Hear that?"

Johnny heard a rising wind. He knew that Mergal had called up another storm, like the one he had summoned on the Fourth of July. "Very impressive," said the professor. "Although I don't see what good it does you."

The small window in the door rapidly darkened. Then a flash of lightning and a furious peal of thunder shook the whole place. "It does me this much good," said Mergal. "I will send these children out, one at a time, and the lightning will take them. Then you can follow them."

"But only I can tell you where the hand is," replied the professor.

"I really don't care anymore. Once you are gone, I will simply buy your house—I'm quite wealthy—and take it apart, plank by plank and brick by brick. I needed the hand by the beginning of next month, but I can wait another year if I must. I have waited all my life." He pointed his long, bony finger at Sarah. "You, girl. Leave now. The other two will watch. They will see how far you get."

Another blast of lightning and thunder made Sarah scream. Then the professor grabbed the hand and held it out. "Why wait?" he asked Mergal. "If you want the hand, here it is. Take it—if you can!"

"Ah!" Mergal's eyes lit with an evil glow. He leaped forward, his right hand outstretched—

The professor danced back, tauntingly. "Run to the door!" he shouted. "Be ready to head for cover!"

The crow leaped off Mergal's shoulder and swooped at them. Sarah swatted at it backhand, and she hit it. The bird squawked and tumbled. Johnny and Sarah ran to the door and hauled it open. The day outside was frighteningly dark—until a bolt of lightning flashed to earth just outside.

Johnny dimly heard the professor chanting strange, outlandish words. Then he saw the old man toss the hand to Mergal. Johnny saw Mergal whirling and spinning madly. He had caught the wooden hand in his own left hand, and it must have clutched him in its fierce grip.

Mergal screamed and reeled, dropping his staff, as the professor ran toward the door.

A swirling black whirlpool opened in the air behind Mergal. The wooden hand tugged him toward the darkness. Johnny heard Mergal's high-pitched, terrified shrieks. Then the darkness engulfed the wizard. At that moment the professor yelled, "Run for it!" All three of them spilled out of the church. As they reached the street, a tremendous blast of lightning, the biggest yet, smashed into the church. The shock knocked them off their feet.

Johnny rolled over, his ears ringing. The black clouds roiled overhead, then began to dissipate with magical speed. The roof of the old church was on fire. The flames spread terrifically fast, sparks flying like magic to the gray house a quarter mile away. Fire raced up its sides, gnawed at its pillars and gingerbread decorations. With a *whump!* the windows blew out, and orange fire began to pour from the empty frames.

The professor stood on tottering legs and helped Johnny and Sarah up. "It's over," he said. "Thank God, it's over now."

Johnny was sobbing. Sarah turned and buried her face against the professor's shirt, and he awkwardly patted her shoulder. People were coming out of their houses to gawk at the blaze. From town came the screams of sirens. The fire trucks were on their way.

CHAPTER EIGHTEEN

"Here we are. Drive on, Macduff!" said the professor, slamming the passenger-side door of Father Higgins' big Oldsmobile.

It was a sunny day in mid-August. Fergie had returned from Ohio, had met Sarah—and after a short time decided he liked her just fine—and then Professor Childermass announced he was treating everyone to a baseball game in Fenway Park. They piled into Father Higgins' car, with Father Higgins, the professor, and Dr. Charles Coote in the front seat and the kids in the back.

"Now that we're under way, finish your story," said Dr. Coote, a mild, reedy man with a fluff of white hair, a long, bent nose, and thick horn-rimmed spectacles. "You were telling us, Roderick, that Mr. Mergal burst in on you unexpectedly." Dr. Coote really did not care very much about baseball, but he was interested in the tale of Mattheus Mergal, which the professor had been spinning out a little at a time.

The professor nodded. "Indeed I was. Mergal surprised me as I was having lunch. He somehow hypnotized me and took me away in his car, but he couldn't find the hand. You see, when things began to get really frightening, I concealed the relic in the chimney, and then I worked out the secret message and wrote the card to John, leaving it with Father Higgins just in case anything happened to me. When Mergal ordered me to tell him someone respectable to whom he could type a false note, I chose Higgy, and I even slipped in a reminder about the card."

"And was the hand hollow, as you suspected?" asked Father Higgins.

"Hollow?" echoed Johnny. "I thought it was carved from a single block."

The professor shrugged. "It looked that way, but it actually was only a thin shell. It had to be. And it was not *carved*, but rather created by magic. Esdrias Blackleach somehow managed to cut off his own left hand—"

"Cool!" whispered Fergie.

"And thrust it inside the hollow wooden shell," continued the professor, ignoring him. "Blackleach then sealed the wrist end of the shell so cunningly that no one could see a seam. His flesh-and-blood hand was now inside the wooden one."

"Why?" asked Sarah. "Was he crazy?"

The professor snorted. "Crazy like a fox! He had found a spell that would allow someone—perhaps his son—to use the hand to resurrect his spirit. He wanted to live again and enjoy the ill-gotten fruits of his wizardry. For just as I suspected, Blackleach was the one real magician in Massachusetts in the year 1692." With a sickly grin, the professor said, "John, you remember the hideous dreams you described. I had a few myself, as I told you. It's clear to me now that Mattheus Mergal used old Blackleach's mirror to haunt us."

After a moment's thought Johnny nodded. "You know," he said, "I was almost convinced that it was Eddie Tompke up to no good. But that was a trick to keep me from blaming Mergal, wasn't it?"

"Bingo!" said the professor. "And Blackleach did the same thing in Salem Village. He sent dreams, or hallucinations, or whatever they were, to victims like Samuel Parris' daughter and niece. They thought the people they saw in these terrible visions were witches, and they accused these people of witchcraft. Imagine the wicked joy that Blackleach felt when no one suspected him of anything!"

"What a repulsive man," said Dr. Coote. "And so the spell I found in the old grimoire did the trick, did it?"

"Indeed it did, Charley," returned the professor. "You were right about the necromantic charm Mergal wished to use for his resurrection. The catch was that the incantation would work on only one day in the year, on the anniversary of Blackleach's death."

"On August first, Lammas Day," said Johnny.

"Quite right. So Mergal was facing a deadline. But there was something else Charley discovered that I believe Mergal completely missed: Chanting the spell on *any* day opened the gates between Life and Death. But it was only on Lammas Day that the Life side would be stronger, and the spirit of old Blackleach would be pulled through to inhabit Mergal's body. If you did the chant on any other day, the Death side of the equation was stronger. I said the chant on July 27, four days too early. So the hand locked onto Mergal and pulled him through the gate. Blackleach did not come into the world of the living, but Mergal passed, body and soul, into the realm of the dead."

Fergie blinked. "Boy," he said. "That's scary."

The professor's voice became somber: "Not as scary as what Mergal would have done if he had succeeded in drawing Blackleach's spirit into his body. For all his wickedness, Blackleach was very small-minded. All he wanted was to get rich at his neighbors' expense. Mergal was another kettle of tainted squid. The man had delusions of grandeur. He imagined himself as Emperor of the World, and he would have tried to carry out his ambitions if he had succeeded in his nefarious scheme. I, for one, would not care to sample the kind of world that such a twisted man would have forged for himself."

"Are we safe?" Sarah asked. "Could Mergal come back here?"

"Yes, we are perfectly safe, and no, he cannot return," said the professor. To Dr. Coote he said, "By the way, Mergal had an assistant in Boston, a weak little man named Crouder. He was the one who occupied Mergal's hotel room and pretended to be Mergal when the authorities began to look into his whereabouts. They haven't arrested him, because he was just a dupe who gave his boss an alibi. But the police did discover a set of lock picks and nearly all the missing artifacts from the museum in a basket Mergal had placed in his car trunk. Even Miss Ferrington had to admit that John was innocent, and she offered him his job again."

"I didn't take it," Johnny said. "I would have to quit when school starts anyway, and I didn't much want to work in the museum anymore."

"Well," said Professor Childermass, "the police released the stuff that Mergal stole from the musem to me. I had Father Higgins come over with holy water and scripture to bless the whole kit and caboodle, and then we disposed of it in a bonfire. Someone kick me if I ever clutter my house with such tomfool gimcracks and geegaws again."

They arrived at Fenway Park and watched an exciting Red Sox–Yankees game. It was a close contest, but when the Yankees came to bat at the top of the ninth, the Red Sox led four to two. They easily put the first two Yankee batters out. That was when the professor stood up and started to razz the Yankees in a loud, obnoxious voice that startled Sarah, delighted Fergie, and embarrassed Johnny.

The Yankee player at the plate was the young slugger Mickey Mantle. He took a couple of practice swings, ignoring the professor's shouted insults. The Red Sox pitcher went into his stretch and put a fastball over high and hard.

Crack! Mantle hit the ball and it soared away. "Oh, you dirty dog!" yelled the professor. "That's a home run!"

It was a very long home run. Mantle trotted around the bases. But the next Yankee batter struck out, and the game ended with the Red Sox winning four to three. Professor Childermass made his way down toward the field, and when he was close enough, he yelled, "You! Number seven!"

"Oh, gosh," groaned Johnny. "He's gonna get in a fight!"

"Yes, you!" bellowed the professor. He tipped his battered old fedora. "Well played, sir! Very well played!"

The surprised Yankee fielder grinned shyly. "Boy, Prof," said Fergie, sounding astonished. "I've never heard you say a kind word for a Yankee until today."

"Byron," returned the professor quietly, "one can always recognize ability and talent in one's adversaries." He raised his voice to a roar: "Especially when the poor dumb Yankees are six and a half games behind the Cleveland Indians!"

All the Red Sox fans around the professor looked at him and chuckled. He beamed and tipped his hat right and left, and even Father Higgins and Dr. Coote joined in the laughter. Johnny, Fergie, and Sarah laughed too, and then they joined the stream of people leaving the ballpark under the clean, bright afternoon sky.

John Bellairs is the critically acclaimed, best-selling author of many Gothic novels, including *The Curse of the Blue Figurine*; *The Mummy, the Will, and the Crypt*; *The Lamp from the Warlock's Tomb*; *The Spell of the Sorcerer's Skull*; and the novels starring Lewis Barnavelt, Rose Rita Pottinger, and Mrs. Zimmermann: *The House With a Clock in Its Walls*; *The Figure in the Shadows*; *The Letter, the Witch, and the Ring*; *The Ghost in the Mirror*; and *The Doom of the Haunted Opera*. John Bellairs died in 1991.

Brad Strickland completed several of John Bellairs's novels, including *The Ghost in the Mirror*; *The Vengeance of the Witch-Finder*; *The Doom of the Haunted Opera*; and *The Drum, the Doll, and the Zombie*. He lives in Oakwood, Georgia.